THE CHRISTMAS MESSENGER

Remembering the Sacredness of Christmas and Living a Christ-Centered Life

By
Shelley Wood

Copyright © 2009 by Shelley Wood

THE CHRISTMAS MESSENGER
by Shelley Wood

Printed in the United States of America

ISBN 978-1-60791-854-7

All rights reserved solely by the author. The author guarantees all contents are original and do not infringe upon the legal rights of any other person or work. No part of this book may be reproduced in any form without the permission of the author. The views expressed in this book are not necessarily those of the publisher.

Unless otherwise indicated, Bible quotations are taken from the King James Version.

www.xulonpress.com

This book is dedicated to my parents
for their love and support throughout my life.

PREFACE

Writing is placing one word after another until the picture is focused. Good writing completes the picture. Shelley Wood is a good writer. One can sense and feel the anticipatory events as they unfold. There are spiritual things that mean more than the infusing of the descriptive adjectives. The author uses this talent to lead the reader. She probes the scope of her work in simplistic tones, yet the innate depth of the work looks toward the redemption of all humankind though the birth and atonement of Jesus Christ.. This is an enjoyable book worth reading.

Jim Faulkner, author and playwright

INTRODUCTION

During my 30 year career as a physician assistant providing primary medical care in five states, a variety of patients have shared special experiences with me. Their experiences, as well as those from family and friends, have inspired this book. The two main characters, Emma Seligmann and Kristen Mathews, are composites of several women. Emma's extraordinary spiritual event related in Chapter Five is based on two patients who shared their own scared experiences with me.

Squeak is a real kitty who was adopted by a friend of mine, Marilyn, when the kitten appeared on her porch hungry and homeless. Squeak's picture on the front cover occurred spontaneously after she had been racing around the living room. She really did climb onto the walnut table by herself and settle behind the manager without knocking over any ceramic figurines!

Many friends have willingly offered their expertise evaluating my manuscript. To them, I offer sincere gratitude for their time, insights, assistance and encouragement.

During my medical career, I've been impressed with fragility of life. From the operating room, to the emergency department, to the clinic, to my own neighborhoods, I've witnessed how the amazing transition from life to death can happen quickly and unpredictably—from infants to aged people alike. Although we mourn the deaths of those who touched our lives, as Christians we have faith that the atoning sacrifice of Jesus Christ in Gethsemane and His resurrection give us the expectation of life-after-death .My hope is that readers will feel inspired by the experiences in this book and desire to come closer to God.

Chapter One

A Work In Progress

"Code 99, ICU"! The terse announcement from the intercom throughout Valley Hospital didn't bother any patients or visitors who were unaware of the secret meaning of 'Code 99'. They wouldn't know that a life versus death struggle was already taking place because a patient's heart had just stopped beating. For Kristen Mathews, an intensive care nurse and a member of the Code Team designated to respond to all cardiac arrests that day, this code also had another meaning.

"So much for lunch today" she thought somewhat begrudgingly. Kristen had just sat down to her meal, after five hours of nonstop nursing care for her patients in the Medical Intensive Care Unit—abbreviated as MICU in medical jargon. Carrying her lunch back to the MICU unit wasn't an option because time was too critical. Kristen briskly pushed herself from the table, ignored her growling stomach, and ran out of the cafeteria. Her quick departure was ignored by the rest of the staff, who were accustomed to such events. A few visitors stopped their conversations and watched curiously as Kristen was joined by a man, dressed in a scrub suit and wearing a white consultation coat. To those in the know, the knee length consultation coat distinguished Dr. Robert Strong as having graduated from the short white coats worn by medical students. One of his white coat pockets bulged with a condensed version of the medical

classic titled <u>Harrison's Textbook of Medicine</u>—unlike some of his colleagues who were well enough off to have the expensive but compact electronic version. His other pocket bulged with a small black notebook that was jokingly referred to as a 'peripheral brain' by resident physicians because it was crammed with diligently acquired notes about diagnosing and treating various medical conditions during internship.

As they both rushed to the nearest stairwell, Rob's fine, blond hair cascaded over his forehead and almost down to his light blue eyes. He brushed his hair back, which lasted only for a moment. "Any ideas as to who arrested?" Rob asked Kristen.

"Of course, in the MICU, there are several possibilities. But, my guess is that Mr. Thompson is at the highest risk of having a cardiac arrest. He was transferred here yesterday from a rural hospital and has been unstable since admission despite everything we've done."

While jogging up the four flights of stairs, Kristen's long auburn hair that was styled into a classic French braid bobbed gently on her neck. By the time they reached the fourth floor, both she and Rob were winded. Nonetheless, they kept jogging through the corridor to the MICU, where they waited for a couple of seconds until the automatic glass doors slid open. They could see through well-placed windows into most of the MICU patient rooms, and rushed into the one room with staff crowded inside around Mr. Thompson's bed. Kristen inwardly groaned when she saw that Dr. Bennett was leading the code. *"Rats! I hope that he can stay more controlled this time than he was last week when he was leading a code,* she thought while squeezing in next to the bright red emergency cart. Immediately Kristen began charging the defibrillator in case it would be needed, as it usually was.

The team worked together, combining modern medical technology with the standard chest compressions that evolved from the 1960's. "Get that timing right" barked Dr. Bennett to the intern doing the chest compressions and the medical student using a respirator. To another medical student whose eyes were fixated on the cardiac monitor, he demanded, "What rhythm is the patient in?"

As the student looked intently at the glowing, jagged lines on the monitor, she answered hesitantly "Ventricular fibrillation?"

"OK, we're short on time here, so call it v-fib. You know that the patient's heart is quivering in a deadly pattern." Looking at Kristen he barked louder than needed in the small room, "Get ready to shock him at 200 hundred joules!"

With her many years of experience in the MICU, Kristen knew what to do and had already adjusted the defibrillator to 200 joules. She quickly removed the charged paddles and held them out to Dr. Bennett. He grabbed the paddles, placed them on the patient's chest, and yelled, "Everyone clear now!"

Quickly everyone stepped away from the patient's bed so that they wouldn't get shocked, and then Dr. Bennett pressed a red button on the handle of one paddle. That instantly sent a strong electrical charge through the patient's heart. As a result of this surge of electricity, the patient's lifeless body jolted. Although this seemingly frantic act would appear to be a hopeless undertaking, it often successfully stimulated the heart into a normal rhythm—at least in hospitalized patients where the presence of emergency equipment and staff allow for a prompt response. All eyes of the staff in the room were riveted on the cardiac monitor to see if a normal heart rhythm appeared. "Still v-fib. Get ready to shock him again but this time at 300 joules!"

Kristen could feel the tension mounting in the room and in her own muscles. Once again her experience had prepared her for what was needed, so she'd already set the defibrillator to 300 joules and had recharged the paddles. Again she handed the paddles without delay to Dr. Bennett. As he grabbed them, he yelled, "Everyone clear now!" Beads of sweat dripped down from his furrowed forehead.

"I want one milligram of epinephrine now!" he barked to Anna, another nurse standing by the red emergency cart. The cart contained several drawers with lifesaving drugs and Anna was familiar with each one of them. However, in her haste, she inadvertently dropped the vial of epinephrine it to the floor where it shattered. In was an innocent mistake that anyone could have made. However, Dr. Bennett didn't see it that way.

"If you can't handle the pressure, get out of here!" he bellowed angrily. The tension was nearly palpable. Another nurse, Karen, quickly retrieved another vial of epinephrine, drew up one milligram, and injected the drug into the patient's intravenous line. Dr. Bennett glared at Anna as she opened the door and left the room. Kristen's own gut tightened and she gritted her teeth to keep her rising anger within.

The team continued the chest compressions and respirations in silence as they watched the heart monitor. After what seemed longer, but was only a moment, the patient's heart ceased fibrillating. "Okay, give him a bolus of lidocaine, and no one drop this one," commanded Dr. Bennett caustically. Karen drew up a syringe of lidocaine. Kristen was amazed to see Karen's hands slightly trembling. *I've never seen Karen so nervous before!*

After a moment, the patient's rhythm returned to a normal pattern. "Okay, it's over. Everyone get back to work "demanded Dr. Bennett sternly as he wiped the sweat off his forehead.

The medical and nursing staff left the patient's room in silence. Kristen felt a sense of relief that Mr. Thompson survived. But Dr. Bennett's acrimonious behavior bothered her. *Successfully resuscitating a patient is so rare, that the code team leader always thanks the team for their work. I can't believe the audacity of Dr. Bennett. It's as though he thinks he did it all by himself!*

The intense flurry of activity dissipated, amidst the normal sounds of monitors beeping, phones ringing, and people talking. Kristen went to the adjacent nurses' locker room, and found her 'emergency' chocolate candy bar in her purse. Ravenous, she consumed it hurriedly as she hurried back to her patients.

Her next patient, Samuel Smith, a 78-year old man recovering from a heart attack, had just awakened from a nap. He was oblivious to the commotion of the cardiac arrest. Seeing Kristen in his room, he sat up and put on his wire-rimmed glasses. Samuel smiled and asked congenially, "Well, how's my favorite nurse doing?"

Relieved that Mr. Thompson is still around! Kristen thought. But she didn't want Samuel to become stressed about another patient's close call with death. "Just fine and thanks for your concern. But I'm concerned that you didn't eat much lunch. You really must remember that you need nourishment to regain your strength."

"Gosh, you sound so much like my dear wife, Mildred. If she were still alive, she'd be here saying the same thing, you know."

Samuel gently pulled Kristen's left hand toward him and looked at it. "No wedding ring? How could a wonderful girl like you not be married?"

Kristen knew Samuel well enough to understand that his question was one of genuine concern. Still, questions about marriage and children only intensified the pain that she felt at never having the opportunity to marry and have a family. Over the years, Kristen and her single friends had discussed their situation countless times. When needed, they consoled themselves with the pithy but true fact they had witnessed in many ways: "There are worse things in life than being single."

But Kristen didn't believe that Samuel would understand their consolatory phrase. She decided to use another fact that her single friends had addressed. "The problem is that there are more single women than men."

"Oh, come on now—"

Kristen interrupted, which she seldom did, especially with her patients. But marriage was a touchy subject. "Just think about this. If boys survive their wild antics of adolescence and young adulthood—such as diving off cliffs, driving too fast, playing with guns and driving drunk—they're often then sent to fight a war. My parents' fathers fought in World War I. My dad and his two brothers fought in World War II. I had uncles who fought in the Korean War. My older sister had classmates who fought in Vietnam, and some never returned. And the wars continue."

"Well, I've never really thought about it that way. Wars certainly kill a lot of good men, and many others as well. I had numerous ancestors involved in wars. As for myself, I was in the Buffalo soldiers' 370th Regimental Combat unit during World War II. Thought I was going to die many times and I almost did die from a gunshot to my chest. That's how I got my big scar, as well as a Purple Heart." Samuel suddenly became quiet and seemingly pensive with his furrowed brow.

"I'm sorry, Samuel. I really didn't mean to depress you. And I didn't know that you were a part of that famous African-American infantry. It's such a privilege to know someone from that brave group who fought so valiantly. I apologize if my chatter brought bad memories for you," Kristen said softly.

"Oh, don't you worry. I was just caught up in the dichotomy of it all. There's the horrible hell that war generates. Yet, we wouldn't be enjoying life in the greatest democratic nation on Earth without our own American Revolution. And the Civil War ended the tyranny of slavery, forever transforming this nation. My ancestors, family and I of course have always been grateful beyond words for the privilege of the freedom won by the bravery of so many who fought to abolish slavery. However, I pray that we'll find a better way to resolve conflict than by sending men and women into war."

"Amen to that. I couldn't agree more."

"But back to you being single. What about that handsome Dr. Strong? He's also a terrific doctor."

Kristen laughed out loud. "Sorry to laugh, but most young men aren't interested in dating women the age of their mother!"

"Oh, come on now. You sure don't look old enough to be his mother."

"Well, I could be if I started young. But thanks for the compliment! Now I need to give you your heart medication, and then start some IV's and pass medications to my other patients. You understand I'm sure. Anything else you need?"

"No, I'm getting along just fine. Can't wait to get out of here though. Don't get me wrong. You're a wonderful girl and a great nurse, as well as the rest of the nurses here. But I sure want to be home in time to have Christmas with my children and their children."

Kristen bristled and gritted her teeth at once again being called a 'girl'. *I can't understand why this generation would never refer to these young male interns as 'boys' but still call us nurses 'girls'! Oh well.* She took a deep breath and went on. "We'll do whatever we can to help. We hope to transfer you to the step-down unit tomorrow, where the nurses can still monitor your heart, but it's not as intense or as noisy as here. You can help by eating some more of your lunch. Okay?"

There was a definite pause as Samuel looked at his meal tray while Kristen's empty stomach growled. "Okay, I'll work on it. But even I can cook better than this, and that isn't saying much!"

As Kristen went from patient to patient, starting intravenous lines, injecting medications, and giving pills, she felt a throbbing migraine headache start. *Just what I don't need today is a headache, on top of everything else. I should have learned by now to not substitute a chocolate candy bar for a meal. And I must learn to deal with stress better. Guess I'll just have to suffer for now.*

Her next patient was a 63-year old woman, Emma Seligmann, who had a high fever, pneumonia, and a worrisome irregular heart rhythm. She was in an isolation room because of her fever, which was higher than usual for pneumonia. So anyone needing to enter Emma's room had to put on a protective yellow gown over their clothing before going in. Upon leaving, they then would remove the gown just outside the room and bag it, in order to protect others. After putting on a yellow gown, Kristen entered Emma's room, drew up an antibiotic solution into a syringe and then injected it into Emma's IV line. Although Kristen worked quietly, the sounds awakened Emma. "Oh, hello, Kristen," she said softly with her ever present smile.

Despite her throbbing head, Kristen managed a smile. "You're always so cheerful and kind, no matter what time of day or night we awaken you."

"Having an 'attitude of gratitude' is one of those important choices in life. And choosing to be grateful brings great joy. Does that make sense?"

Kristen smiled wryly. "Well, most people aren't grateful about being a patient in the MICU, especially during the Christmas season."

Emma smiled. "However, from my point of view, I'm grateful to have good nurses like you caring for me. And I can celebrate Christ's birth anywhere," Emma explained patiently.

Kristen nodded her head in understanding. "Well, that does make sense. However, I'll have to do some work to achieve an 'attitude of gratitude'. But thanks for sharing that thought."

"Most of the significant skills that we learn require practice, whether learning to ride a bicycle or playing a musical instrument. So be patient with yourself. Well, have they determined what bacteria are causing my pneumonia, and if my fever is secondary to anything else yet?"

"No, the blood and sputum culture results are still pending. How do you feel?"

"Like I wrestled with a bear. Just no energy left. You on the other hand look like you're getting a headache. Am I right?"

Kristen was baffled. "How could you know?"

Emma smiled. "I've been a nurse myself for four decades, and I've learned to pick up on subtle cues. Also, I learned a lot about overcoming pain because of a car wreck in my 20's and cancer in my 60's. Besides, I heard the 'Code 99' being paged to the MICU. Those are emotionally draining and stressful."

"Especially when you're dealing with some difficult physicians, as you surely understand."

Emma chuckled. "Oh, yes. I remember years ago when as a nurse we were expected to give up our chair at the nurse's station for any doctor who happened to come along, even if we had been on our feet for hours. That's improved, fortunately. Over the years, I've learned to accept that all of us are imperfect, but still beloved, children of God. When I'm bothered by someone's behavior, I just refer to him as 'a work in progress'. It's then easier to just forget the incident."

"'A work in progress.' Well, that's an interesting way to look at irritating behavior!"

"It's certainly cut down on my headaches. Another piece of wisdom that I learned years ago was an adage from a friend that goes, 'He who angers you, conquers you.' That wise-saying has reminded me to maintain control of my emotions."

"That's a great adage!" Kristen grinned. "But do you have any magic formulas for dealing with arrogant physicians?" asked Kristen in a mildly sarcastic tone.

"Actually, I've found the sandwich technique to be helpful working with all kinds of undesirable behaviors. First you praise him. Then you calmly state the desired behavior. Then you praise him again. Works like a charm—most of the time, any way."

"The 'sandwich technique'. Well, it sounds like it's worth a try." Kristen smiled, and then winced, as her headache throbbed even more intensely.

Emma reached out and gently touched Kristen's hand. "Please let me teach you a technique that's helped relieve me of my headaches over the years. Can you spare five minutes?"

Kristen felt awkward. She was supposed to be caring for Emma. "Well this is certainly a new experience for me. I'm the nurse here for you."

"But this will help you through the rest of the work that you need to do. Remember, I'm a nurse, too."

Kristen finally nodded in agreement, as she felt her headache throbbing. Emma gently instructed her. "Now stand with your spine in good alignment, and clasp your hands together behind your neck. Bring your elbows back." Kristen followed Emma's directions. "That's right. Now let your head rest against your hands, which will allow your chin to tilt upward. Good. And now take a couple of deep, diaphragmatic breaths, feeling your chest and abdomen expand with your breath." As Kristen followed Emma's directions, she found herself relaxing despite her headache. Then Emma soothingly described a tranquil scene on a beach, with warm sunshine, a gentle breeze, and ocean waves lapping the white sand.

After a few minutes, Emma gently asked, "How do you feel, Kristen?"

Kristen opened her eyes and paused for a moment. "I'm truly amazed! My headache is almost completely gone. Even medication doesn't work this fast. "

"I've learned through several surgeries, and through some painful life experiences that we have tremendous power within ourselves to overcome much of the tribulations of life. You've just felt it yourself."

"I can't thank you enough.."

"You're doing a lot to care for me. The least I can do is to help relieve your pain."

Kristen slowly made her way to the bedside table where she had left her medication tray. She had so many questions to ask Emma, but she had other patients to care for. For the first time she noticed on Emma's bedside table a small hurricane lamp with its gleaming gold base. Within the six inch sparkling glass chimney was a gold candle. Emma saw Kristen gazing at the lamp. "I bring that with me wherever I go, as a reminder of where I've been and what I've learned. But that's a long story." Emma paused as she studied Kristen's face. "Maybe when you have some free time and I have some more strength, I'll share it with you, if you're interested."

Kristen looked with esteem and wonder at this woman who had been just another patient until a few minutes ago. "Does this lamp have anything to do with your surgeries after your car accident or cancer?"

"It certainly does," replied Emma with a smile.

Hearing a buzzer go off in an adjacent patient's room jarred Kristen out of her preoccupied state. She grabbed the medication tray, and on her way out of the room responded, "Thanks again for the headache cure. And yes I would love to hear your story. Perhaps we'll have time tomorrow."

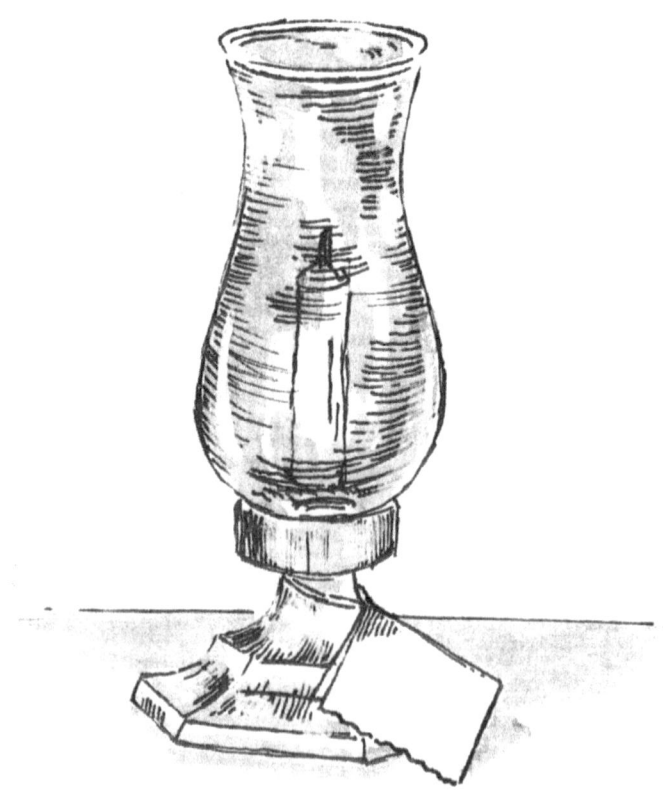

THE CHRISTMAS MESSENGER

Her nursing work almost completed, Kristen wearily finished typing notes about each of her patients in a rather cramped 'computer room' behind the nurses' station. There nurses and resident physicians typed patients' charts at half a dozen computers. Some typed quickly, and others less so with a limited two-index-finger technique. Finally finished, she stretched and said a "goodbye" to those in the computer room, and then to the nurses and clerk busy at the nurses' station. Leaving the MICU, she saw Anna slowly walking towards the women's locker room. Kristen sped up her pace, and gently put her arm around Anna's shoulders. "You know, Anna, you're a great nurse. And it's easier to let that incident go, by remembering that Dr. Bennett is a child of God, as well as he's 'a work in progress'."

The tension in Anna's face eased and she chuckled. "You're right. He's definitely a work in progress! But do you really think he'll progress past this stage?"

"With our help! Besides, our patient survived, which beats the odds any way. So at least that's in his favor."

Anna nodded in agreement. "Surviving a cardiac arrest certainly does beat the odds. But as far as helping this egotistical physician progress, I'll let you begin first."

Kristen laughed. "Thanks a lot. I'll see what I can do. Maybe I'll get some divine inspiration," she said, but inwardly doubting that was even possible.

Outside the hospital in the bitter cold, Kristen dashed past the row of trees separating the parking lot from the hospital. *"Trees are so ugly with their barren branches. Can't wait for spring, when the weather warms up and trees are covered with green leaves again."*

Through the traffic was heavy, there were no accidents to circumvent on the way home. One driver however, did cut in front of Kristen forcing her to brake suddenly. Kristen cursed loudly. Then she remembered Emma's saying: "He who angers you, conquers you."

Kristen sighed out loud as she recalled another of Emma's lessons. "Alright, so he's a work in progress. Hope he progresses rapidly, before it's too late." Immediately, she found herself relaxing some, rather than tensing up more as she usually did.

THE CHRISTMAS MESSENGER

Finally reaching her home, Kristen tiredly opened the front door to her apartment. Kicking off her shoes, she plopped down on her dark green recliner. "Sure would be nice if someone would cook dinner for me," she said wryly in her almost empty apartment. Kristen's pure white kitten, Squeak, awakened from her nap and scampered from the bedroom. She jumped onto Kristen's lap. Stretching herself full length, she reached up and licked Kristen's neck. Kristen stroked her soft white fur gently. "For a stray, you're so friendly. Even if you can't cook dinner for me, you've been a sweet companion ever since I first heard you squeaking so plaintively on my front porch."

Squeak settled down expectantly in Kristen's lap. As Kristen continued stroking her, Squeak purred contentedly. That tranquil scene lasted only for a couple of minutes. Then she jumped down, and began racing around the room, dashing across the sofa, climbing into the large potted plant on the floor, and knocking over an empty glass on the end table.

"Will you ever out-grow your frenzied exploring and knocking things over?"

Squeak looked momentarily at Kristen, and "meowed" in response. Then she began quickly circling around and fervently chasing her tail. Kristen couldn't help but to laugh.

However, she was also tired and hungry. Wearily picking up the glass from the floor, she turned on the television, and shuffled into the kitchen. Squeak raced ahead of her into the kitchen and stood by her food dish. Her tail twitched in excitement and she meowed loudly. "Okay, okay. You should know by now that I'll feed you first," Kristen replied, as she opened a can of kitten food and scooped it into Squeak's dish. Squeak ate voraciously, while Kristen pondered her own dinner. Too tired to cook, she resorted to heating a frozen dinner fried chicken in the microwave. "Squeak, with the headache I've already had today, guess I'd better settle for a cup of hot peppermint tea although I'd rather have my favorite of hot chocolate."

With a steaming cup of peppermint tea in one hand and her dinner in the other, Kristen returned to the living room settled back into her recliner. Squeak bounced up onto her lap, and nestled down for a nap. Clicking through the channels, Kristen chose a popular movie. But she felt more and more depressed as she watched the racy scenes of a couple who'd just met. "This sure isn't what I ever envisioned about 'true love'," Kristen said to Squeak, who was purring contentedly, while curled up on her lap. "I hope that there's more to life and love than what Hollywood portrays. My parents weren't devoutly religious, but they still taught my sister and me to be moral in our conduct. They made it clear to us that they didn't have intimate relationships before marriage because it was important to obey God's commandments. They were faithfully and happily married for decades before they died." Kristen sighed and went into the kitchen. Squeak quickly followed. "Squeak, you can't understand how disheartening life is. And when we humans get discouraged, we like to eat. So I'm having a banana split," explained Kristen as she retrieved a carton of ice cream from her freezer. As she sliced the banana, she gave some to Squeak who licked inquisitively at the new food. She squeezed some chocolate topping onto of the ice cream and then some whipped cream to complete the dessert.

Settling down with her banana split, Kristen hoped the movie would improve. But it didn't. Kristen licked the final bite off her spoon. Feeling stuffed, disgusted with the movie, and still depressed, she turned off the TV before the movie ended.

"Squeak, I just don't understand why people rush into bed. I've always felt that any intimate relationship was so special that it should be saved for marriage. That's what love and romance have always meant to my family: saving intimacy for marriage, being faithful to your spouse, and loving your children. But any more, that kind of love seems so idealistic that it seems unrealistic in our current society."

Kristen picked up Squeak and gently put her in her cat bed in the corner of her bedroom. After showering, and brushing her teeth, Kristen crawled into her own bed. But she couldn't sleep. Tossing and turning, she wondered about the events of the day: Mr. Thompson's near-death, Dr. Bennett's angry behavior, the endless work in the ICU, the craziness of drivers on the highway, Hollywood's version of romance, and even the real meaning of life.

Squeak wasn't ready to sleep. After playing around the room for awhile, she jumped up on Kristen's bed and snuggled next to her. As she stroked Squeak, Kristen remembered Emma's hurricane lantern. "You know, Squeak, I met the nicest woman today. She has this beautiful lamp that's been with her during her many surgeries and treatments. I don't want to get my hopes up, but maybe her story will reveal some meaning to life. Perhaps Emma will share that with me tomorrow."

With these contemplative thoughts, Kristen found herself relaxing. From her kitten's quiet breathing, she could tell that Squeak was already asleep. Within moments, Kristen began sleeping peacefully as well.

CHAPTER TWO

"Life isn't Fair, but God's Love is Always There."

The sound of her bedside alarm jolted Kristen out of a deep sleep. "It's too early," she groaned, while pushing the snoozer button. Ten minutes later, the alarm rang again. This time, Squeak began licking her face and meowing loudly in her ear. "Alright, I'm getting up," Kristen mumbled as she dragged herself out of bed and turned on her bedside lamp. In the dim light, she pulled on a turtleneck and slacks. While half awake, she brushed her hair, and deftly intertwined it into a French braid. Her kitten meowed plaintively as Kristen walked and Squeak pranced their way to the kitchen.

"Okay, okay, here's your breakfast," as she spooned some canned kitten food into Squeak's bowl. Still full from her late night banana split, Kristen decided to skip breakfast. "Today I'm taking some food for later so I don't go hungry like yesterday," she said while stuffing an apple, banana and a couple of granola bars into her back pack. At the front door, she lovingly stroked Squeak. "At least you don't have to go out in the cold. Try to not knock anything over today."

Kristen braced herself against the icy winter wind in the darkness of the early morning. Under the dim light in the parking stall, she fumbled with the key, trying to quickly open the door of her white sedan that was splattered with frozen slush from the last snow storm. *Gosh, I hope there aren't any problems with black ice on the highway. It's so scary to suddenly be sliding out of control just because of a sheet of invisible ice on a black highway.* Finally inside her car, but shivering from the cold, she coaxed the sluggish engine to start. Turning on the radio for some company, Christmas music filled the air. At first, it was a pleasant distraction. But then another song about Christmas romance began playing. Hastily, she shut off the music. *I'm so tired of the commercialization of Christmas. What's so merry about Christmas anyway?* On the highway, a red sports car pulled sharply in front of her, forcing Kristen to brake suddenly. Then she started sliding on the ice. After several terrifying seconds, she managed to get control of her car. However, before cursing as usual, she recalled one of Emma's lessons. "He who angers you, conquers you." She took a deep breath, and tried to relax. *Two near crashes in two days! What's wrong with these drivers? It's like they have a desperate rush to death.*

It was almost seven o'clock when Kristen pulled into the hospital parking lot. Once again, she braced herself against the cold morning air, while walking carefully and trying to avoid patches of ice on the black pavement. After the long and cold walk from the parking lot, she struggled to get the hospital door to open against the wind. Away from the cold, snow and wind, Kristen savored the sensation of the warmth seeping into her muscles. She walked up the four flights and down the corridor to the women's locker room, where she began changing into a teal scrub suit along with other MICU nurses.

"I wonder how our patients are doing, and who made it through the night," pondered Karen as she pulled on her scrubs.

"That's a continual worry in our jobs" responded Rebecca. "Some days, especially when the stress higher than normal and certain people begin yelling, I'd surely rather being doing something less hectic, like selling socks, or maybe being a beach bum in the Caribbean," she said with a grin as she secured her long brown hair in a barrette.

Kristen started laughing so hard that she had to stop tying her white athletic shoes. "Somehow I can't picture you selling socks! However, especially on cold, winter days like today, I'd really like to try the beach scene. But you know that we couldn't stand the serenity for long. Why else would we do this feverish pace day after day?"

Rebecca leaned against the lockers. Still smiling she continued. "I'll bet you lunch—not that we usually have time for such luxuries—that at least once today you'll think about doing something easier! However, there's definitely something about personalities that make's one person want to be in a helping profession and deal with life-and-death situations—like ICU nurses, trauma surgeons, ER nurses and doctors, as well as firefighters, paramedics, and police officers, to name a few."

"Then there's the personalities who are money-driven at what ever cost," added Anna as she combed her curly red hair. "That's definitely not us or we wouldn't be here at these salaries!" They all laughed together in agreement as they walked to the nearby MICU.

Assembling in the conference room, the night shift charge nurse, Esther, reviewed all the patients. "I'm happy to report that no one died last night," Esther began as she tucked her pen into her dark, black hair above her ear. "But of course, that doesn't mean anything for today, as you all know." Each nurse had their own way for coping with the stress of working in the MICU, and dealing with the possibility of their patients going into cardiac arrest or dying some other way. Rebecca, the charge nurse for the day shift, always chewed gum and bounced her foot, as she jotted meticulous notes about each patient. Anna sipped tea from her mug, and doodled on her tablet. Karen deftly cross-stitched Christmas tree ornaments in between jotting down notes on her patients. Patrick, who had just quit smoking, continually chewed on anything—gum, pencils, candy, carrot sticks, and his fingernails. Kristen munched on her apple and drank orange juice while she took notes on her patients.

Esther continued, "Emma Seligmann isn't any better with the current antibiotic. She still has a very high fever and an irregular heart rhythm. Hopefully the test results will come back today so that we can find out what bacteria are causing her pneumonia. And that concludes my report. Have a great day!" she said cheerily. Esther exited the conference room, along with the rest of the nurses.

Kristen was relieved to learn that she had been assigned Emma again. She started a couple of intravenous lines, passed medications and gave some injections. Before entering Emma's room, she donned the yellow gown a d washed her hands. Emma greeted Kristen with her ever-present smile. "Looks like your headache is still gone!"

"Thanks to you," she responded happily as she set the medication tray on the bedside table. "I'll remember to try that the next time I start getting a headache."

Even with her limited view from the window of her room into the hallway, Emma could see some holiday decorations. "Apparently the night shift had time to put up a Christmas tree and lights last night. I always like the merry atmosphere that decorations bring. You know that hospitals can be so dreary."

Kristen nodded her head as she checked Emma's heart rhythm and blood pressure on the monitor. "Well, I certainly agree with you on that."

"Do you celebrate Christmas with your family?"

Kristen paused, not sure how to answer the superficially easy question. "Well, I do celebrate Christmas with my sister and her children and grandchildren." *I'm just not sure what I believe in any more*, she thought while injecting an antibiotic into Emma's intravenous line. Then looking back at Emma, she continued, "What about you?"

"Well, being an only child and a widow, I'm on my own. Thank goodness for friends, especially on holidays."

"That's for sure." Kristen paused for a moment, not wanting to intrude but desiring to learn more about Emma's life. "If you don't mind me asking, how long have you been a widow?"

"No, I don't mind. That was a long, long time ago. Actually, my husband, Henry, and I were driving home from our honeymoon. We were just married the week before. A drunk driver on the other side of the highway lost control of his car. His car suddenly careened across the median and crashed into ours. My husband died immediately."

Kristen gasped in horror as she sank down into the bedside chair.

"Now dear, that was a long time ago when I was 23."

"But that's so tragic! " Kristen was surprised at her own tears.

With a soothing voice, Emma responded, "This life is filled

with challenges. Who are we to know what tragedies God causes to happen, or those he merely permits? For many months I was filled with despair and anger. However, I learned two important lessons. One lesson is that life isn't fair. And the other lesson is that each of us must make many choices in our lives, including whether adversity will be a tragedy that destroys us, or challenge that will make us stronger."

"But what did you do? And how did you cope?"

"Well, what helped me initially, was the comfort I received in the emergency department." Emma's eyes closed, as she recalled the scene.

"What happened?" asked Kristen softly, yearning to know but not wanting to be intrusive.

"I've never known how to explain this except that there was a powerful presence by my side comforting me. I felt my anguish being replaced with peace. I couldn't see anything, but it was so powerful that I presumed there must be an angelic presence."

Kristen looked out the window and rolled her eyes in disbelief. *Here we go again with guardian angels. I don't understand people's fixation with angels! I've been through some rough times, especially when my parents died, but I've never felt like any angels were helping me.*

Emma went on to explain the details of her accident . Her voice was subdued to almost a whisper. "My facial bones were crushed and I had many other fractures. After my first night in the hospital, I saw that elegant hurricane lantern on the bedside table. A note was attached to it, with a beautifully scripted verse. It's still hanging on the lamp, if you want to read it."

Kristen marveled again at the lamp with its shiny gold base and gleaming glass chimney. For the first time, she saw the small white card with its edges painted gold, which was tied to the base of the chimney with a braided gold ribbon. She opened the delicate card and softly read:

'Life isn't fair, but God's love is always there;
Turn to Him, and your pain will dim;
Follow His Light, and you will eternally be right.'

THE CHRISTMAS MESSENGER

Emma continued softly, "Over the years, I've learned how true that verse is." Tears began rolling down her cheeks. With a tissue, she gently wiped them away.

"I'm so sorry. I don't mean to upset you."

"Oh, these are tears of joy!" She smiled as she again brushed away more tears.

"So, who put the lamp on your bedside table?" asked Kristen as she gazed at it.

Emma dabbed at her eyes with a tissue and had another coughing spell. After sipping some orange juice, she continued. "That's always been a mystery. It must have been one of my family or friends, even though they all denied doing so. But I've learned that God often uses his children to help others and to be messengers of his love. Over the ensuing decades I've treasured that lovely lamp, and how it symbolizes Christ as the eternal light for the world. The lamp and poem have been poignant reminders of God's eternal love through some difficult times. This lamp was by my bedside as I went through the twelve hospitalizations for surgery to repair my body and reconstruct my face. I found the scriptures to be a great comfort during my convalescence. Philippians 4:13 became one of my favorites. It's short but so meaningful: "I can do all things through Christ which strengtheneth me."

"That's an awesome verse," said Kristen as she reached for her pen. "Let me jot that down. Perhaps I should dust off my Bible and read it." Emma smiled with a nod of understanding. "But, please continue with your story," she said as she finished writing.

"Well, all those surgeries made it impossible to continue working as a life flight nurse. So I decided to return to college and earn my doctorate in nursing. That also helped fill the void in my life after becoming a widow. Since then, I've taught hundreds of students, and done some clinical nursing as well. It's been a great career..." Her coughing interrupted her sentence.

Kristen handed her the glass of juice. As Emma sipped, she replied, "I think you must have been a great nurse and professor! But I'm surprised that you never remarried."

"Well, I've had a fiancé and a husband both die in accidents. It seemed like the best thing I could do for the male population was to stay single. Besides, when you've only been married a week, you're too in love to get into a tiff over anything. I didn't dare spoil a perfect marriage," she said with a chuckle.

Kristen couldn't help but smile as well. "You are an amazing person! I don't think I could be able to cope as well as you."

"Well, I've found that humor is a great healing balm. Later in life, while I was recuperating from one of my earlier surgeries, one of the many books I read was Norman Cousin's <u>Anatomy of an Illness</u>. It's a great contribution to modern medicine about the power of humor in healing. Have you read it?"

"I've been meaning to read it. That's one of the books in my stack at home," confessed Kristen.

"Well, Norman was able to get relief from his severe pain by watching slap-stick movies that made him laugh passionately. After ten minutes of deep laughter, he would be able sleep for an hour, even without any pain medication."

"Wow, that's incredible! But that doesn't really surprise me because we've learned that jokes here in the ICU to help us cope with the stress. And my single friends like to laugh about our strangest dates when we're feeling depressed about being single. But you have quite a remarkable life story. I'd love to hear more but work calls."

Emma smiled wistfully, and then softly placed her hand over Kristen's. "There was an even more remarkable event later in my life. Someday, when you're ready, I'll share it with you. But now I know that you need to attend to your other patients and I need some rest."

Kristen raised herself out of the bedside chair, and looked again at the hurricane lamp. *I wonder what she means by that. Does she know that I don't exactly buy into this guardian angel stuff?*

"You're right and you look very tired. I'll see you later."

She picked up the medication tray and headed to her next patient. Walking down the hallway, Kristen pondered over the events that Emma had just shared with her. *"I can't even imagine the pain of losing my husband after one week of marriage, in addition to enduring twelve surgeries, and then being treated for cancer. Emma's certainly an extraordinary woman.*

The day turned from a typical hectic day at the MICU, to a very stressful full-house. There were two cardiac arrests followed by three more admissions, filling the unit to full capacity. *On days like this, selling socks actually sounds blissful!* thought Kristen sarcastically. Around one in the afternoon, Kristen felt hunger pangs gnawing at her. She found Anna at the nurse's station charting on her patients. "Hey Anna, I didn't get a chance to take lunch. Can you cover for me long enough to go to the cafeteria and buy a sandwich?"

"Sure. Then you can cover for me. With all the admissions, it's been quite a frenzied day for us! Selling socks would certainly be easier," quipped Anna with a wink.

"I concur," she responded with a grin. "Too bad we don't have time to check that out during our leisurely lunches!" Rather than resorting to eating her granola bars, she dashed to the cafeteria, and returned quickly with her hamburger and fries. Pressed for time, she ate rapidly, in between typing notes on a computer about her patients. In her haste, she dripped some ketchup on the keyboard. *Rats! I've got to switch to something that doesn't drip–or maybe a different job like being a beach bum.* After cleaning up her ketchup mess, she proceeded with the afternoon medications and procedures. Samuel Smith was stable enough to be transferred to the step-down unit. Kristen quickly typed her final charting to transfer him, and then went to see him off.

"Well, Mr. Smith, if you keep doing so well, it looks like you're going to get your wish of being home in time for Christmas," said Kristen cheerfully.

Samuel gently grasped Kristen's hand and kindly kissed it. "Thanks for all you've done."

Kristen clasped her hands around his large hand and smiled. "That's one of the greatest pleasures of this job: helping patients recover so they can return to their homes, and families. I've seen your children here every day, so now you'll get to enjoy Christmas with them and I presume some grandchildren, too. Besides, I had the great honor of meeting a World War II Buffalo soldier. How can I beat that for a rewarding career?" With glistening eyes, Samuel waved goodbye as an orderly wheeled him away in a wheelchair.

Finally her shift was over, her charting completed, and the report to the next shift of nurses concluded. *At last, I can go home and rest my tired body!* As she was getting ready to head out of the MICU, Kristen decided to say goodbye to Emma, who had slept most of the afternoon.

Emma was curled up on her bed, reading her Bible. She smiled as Kristen entered the room. "Just wanted to see you before I left for the day," she said with more energy than she felt.

"Well, thank you. Guess I slept most of the afternoon. I did over hear some nurses talking about your holiday party last weekend. Did you go?"

"No. You know those dinner and dance events are oriented to couples. And they just aren't much fun when you're single."

Emma nodded her head and quietly responded, "Being single in a couples-oriented society is a challenge. I know of two couples who shared Thanksgiving dinner for 25 years. When one of the husbands died, the widow still expected to share Thanksgiving with her friends, but they never invited her again. It was very painful time for her. Later another friend told her that the woman was afraid to share her husband, even once a year for a holiday dinner, out of an irrational fear that she'd lose him. Unfortunately, most of the holiday celebrations from Thanksgiving through New Year's eve are geared towards couples and families."

"That's certainly true. I hate to whine, but even much of the Christmas music is centered on romance and other things that have nothing to do with Jesus."

"Kristen, remember music has a tremendous impact on our emotions, for better or worse."

"Well, you're right of course," replied Kristen thoughtfully. "I've never really thought about how music affects our mood. But there are even music therapists who spend their entire careers using music to help heal people."

Emma nodded in agreement. "That's right! Personally, I'm very selective about the music I listen to all year, but especially during the Christmas season. One of my favorite is a hymn called 'I Heard the Bells on Christmas Day'. Do you know it?" asked Emma.

Kristen paused for a few seconds, trying to recall the hymn. "I think so. Isn't that the one Longfellow wrote in response to the

THE CHRISTMAS MESSENGER

suffering of the Civil War?"

Emma sipped some apple juice before continuing. "Yes, the Civil War, as well as a lot of personal tragedy. His first wife died suddenly, while they were touring in Europe. Several years later, he married Fanny. However, in 1861, Fanny died in a terrible fire. They had been married for 18 years. Longfellow's journal reflects his personal pain from Fanny's tragic death, as well as the many deaths resulting from the Civil War. During the third Christmas season after the loss of Fanny, he received news that his son Charles had been injured in the War—" Emma began coughing.

Kristen glanced at the heart monitor as she handed the cup of juice to Emma. "That's an engrossing story, but perhaps I should go and let you rest. We can continue tomorrow."

Emma shook her head, and then sipped some juice, "Don't worry. I'm almost finished. Finally, on Christmas Day of 1864—the fourth Christmas after Fanny's death and the fourth Christmas of the Civil War—Longfellow wrote the seven-stanza poem, 'Christmas-Bells'. An unknown reviser later converted the poem into a hymn and changed the stanzas. Nevertheless, that poem poignantly reveals his years of personal and national suffering. The last two stanzas focus on peace and righteousness, which should be part of what we focus on at Christmas."

"You must really like that hymn to know so much of its history! I'll listen more closely to the words next time. But besides the music, it seems like the real meaning of Christmas is virtually absent in so much of what we do, from most of the parties to the shopping frenzy."

"Yes, but that need not happen either, Kristen. We can make choices to focus our own lives on the essence of Christmas. The most meaningful gifts come from the heart, such as sharing a special event with our family members and friends. Remember that love is the best and greatest gift we can give."

"That makes a lot of sense, but it's not how our society behaves."

"We can choose to behave differently, through meaningful gifts and through helping those in need, not just at Christmas but throughout the year. Remember that Christmas is a unique religious event. We should celebrate Christmas as God's gift to us because He gave his only begotten Son to us. And then we should celebrate Easter as Christ's gift to us because Jesus gave his life for us—first through atoning for our sins in Gethsemane and then through His death followed by His resurrection. Those who profess to be Christians must understand that without these divine gifts our lives would be meaningless. Equally important is the fact that those incomparable and unsurpassed gifts are given to all of humankind. Remember Kristen that God loves us all unconditionally. And God's help is always present to strengthen and enable us to overcome our flaws and meet every challenge in our lives. However, God allows us the choice to reach out to Him in prayer for that divine witness, guidance and comfort."

Kristen was surprised as she felt tears welling up. She touched Emma's hand. "Thanks. You're a tremendous messenger for God and about the real meaning of Christmas. But, I'd better go now and let you rest." She waved goodbye and Emma waved weakly back.

THE CHRISTMAS MESSENGER

In the locker room, Kristen thought about her conversations with Emma, as she changed into her street clothes. *Don't know what to think about her story about an angel, but what she said about overcoming personal tragedy sure makes sense. And she's right about being selective about Christmas events and even music to make it a meaningful celebration of Christ's birth.*

Outside the hospital, the afternoon sun had warmed the air to a comfortable temperature. The azure blue sky was cloudless. To the east, Kristen saw the beautiful snow-capped mountains. *What a beautiful sight!* She surprised even herself when she impulsively gazed heavenward for a moment.

Driving along the busy streets, she was grateful to have snow and ice melted. On entrance ramp to the freeway, she began accelerating to near highway speed. Just in front of her was a semi-truck, which was also accelerating. Immediately behind her was a line of traffic also restlessly speeding up, all in a rush to get on the highway as fast as possible. Suddenly, Kristen witnessed the two right-rear wheels of the semi-truck come off entirely. Not only was the truck immediately disabled, but also the two wheels were coming directly at Kristen's windshield. She slammed her brake pedal hard to keep from slamming into the truck. Gripping her steering wheel, she felt paralyzed with fear, in part from the terrifying scene of the two large wheels now flying directly towards her windshield. The air was filled with a loud screeching of brakes from the semi-truck, her car and the cars behind, which also added to her fear, causing a rush of adrenalin that resulted in her heart pounding rapidly. *I'm going to be crushed to death!*

Then, by some inexplicable phenomenon, the two wheels that were coming directly towards her windshield suddenly deflected around her car and bounced off the road. By some wonder, Kristen's immediate braking managed to stop her car in time to keep from crashing into the disabled truck stopped in front of her. By some other wonder, the car just behind her screeched to a stop without crushing her into the truck. By another wonder, even though the truck had lost two wheels, the truck driver managed to stop without losing control. By another wonder, the airborne truck wheels rolled off to the sides of the freeway entrance without causing an accident among the crowd of cars rushing behind Kristen on the freeway entrance ramp.

For a moment, it seemed like time froze. Stunned by should have caused a terrible if not a fatal accident, Kristen pulled off onto the emergency lane. Trembling, she rested her head on the steering wheel and recalled the details of the nearly disastrous accident. "This happened so fast! I should have smashed into the semi-truck. That car behind me should have crushed me under that semi. And that semi-truck, after losing its two rear wheels, should have crashed. And I can't understand how those wheels and tires that were headed directly towards my windshield deflected around me!" Her heart was still pounding, and her gut was feeling like it was a mass of knots. "What I just witnessed is impossible! There's too many 'wonders'. So I think that's at least four miracles." Kristen sat back, closed her eyes and took some long, deep breaths. "Maybe there are guardian angels after all," she whispered.

CHAPTER THREE

Choosing Peace by Choosing God

Kristen awakened in the darkness of early morning, long before her alarm went off. Once again, she relived her incredible experience on the highway the night before, as she had already done numerous times since that miraculous event. Shivering from the memory, she felt goose bumps all over. *I should be dead—or at least in critical condition!* Unable to fall asleep again, she went to the kitchen and poured some cereal into a bowl. Turning the TV to the local news, she heard a grim report about a deadly highway accident the night before that resulted in the deaths of an entire family. Squeak snuggled into her lap as she sat on the sofa. Stroking her kitten, she shook her head in disbelief. "It doesn't make sense. Why was my life spared?" she questioned aloud. "Squeak, I can't make sense of this but I wonder what Emma will think?"

Kristen cuddled Squeak in her arms as she returned to her bedroom. With the weatherman's prediction of a wind chill factor below zero, she dressed in her warm gray wool slacks and a heavy sweater. Tenderly stroking her kitten before opening the front door she said quietly, "I know you can't understand me but please try to not break anything while I'm away."

Outside, the stars twinkled and the full moon still shone in the velvet black sky. A harsh and bitterly cold wind immediately enveloped her. Even with her down winter coat zipped, wool neck scarf and hood pulled up, she felt her muscles tighten as she braced herself against the blowing wind and hurried towards her car. As cold as her car was, it was a relief to escape from the frigid wind.

After several minutes of driving in silence, Kristen began to feel some lukewarm air coming from the heating duct in her car. As the car interior began heating up, she began to relax. Far too soon it seemed, she arrived at the entrance ramp to the highway and began to accelerate. Her muscles instinctively tensed as she immediately flashed back to the near collision the night before. Out loud she reprimanded herself. "This is silly! There's no need to tense up. You've driven this highway countless times without any problems. At least there's not much traffic this early in the morning. And there aren't any semi-trucks ahead of you!"

Her self-assessment induced a partial state of calmness. Turning the car radio on, Kristen heard someone gleefully singing about a holiday romance. Hastily she turned off her radio and sighed. *Emma's right. Selecting the right music can help us focus on the real reason for celebrating Christmas. And after last night's experience, I feel greatly indebted to the Lord.*

Kristen arrived ahead of the rest of the nurses. In the silence of the locker room, she changed quickly into some clean scrubs. Entering the MICU, she saw the panel of glowing heart monitors at the nursing station. She searched for Emma's, and saw that her heart tracing was still irregular. Her pulse and respiratory rate continued to be rapid because of the pneumonia and fever. Looking through the glass window into Emma's room, she noted her labored breathing. *Emma, you've been through so much. You can't die now!*

Feeling her eyes brimming with tears, Kristen hurriedly left before the night nurses saw her. Retreating to the cafeteria, she bought a cup of peppermint tea and a banana nut muffin. She took a sip of the hot tea, savoring the warmth. The windows of the cafeteria overlooked the valley, allowing a favorable view of the morning sun, which was just peeking over the mountain tops and creating a beautiful orange glow over the city. Kristen began to unwrap her muffin. For some inexplicable reason, the muffin fell out of its paper wrapper, and broke up into pieces. Nuts and bits of muffin rolled in every direction across the table. A couple of nearby people watched as Kristen worked to clean up the mess.

Embarrassed, she felt her face flushing. "I hope that this isn't a bad omen for the day!" she muttered to herself.

After she had gathered the many pieces of muffin, Kristen looked up, hoping that no one was still watching, but feeling that someone was. At the cashier's station, a man with dark brown, wavy hair was paying for his breakfast and looking directly at Kristen. By his blue scrubs and white consultation coat, Kristen concluded that he was a physician. When their eyes met, he quickly looked away. *That's typical. But he looks vaguely familiar, like someone I knew years ago. He's probably an anesthesiologist. They're the only ones who wear turtlenecks underneath their scrub suits, and have clamps attached to their white coats. But I don't recall knowing any anesthesiologists here. Oh, well. It doesn't matter anyway.*

Kristen finished scooping up her mess and dumped it in the trash can. Still sipping her tea, she walked down the corridor to the stairs. She gazed for a moment at the elevators. *I know that climbing the stairs is good for you, but sometimes I just don't want to.* After a momentary battle, Kristen began climbing the stairs to the fourth floor.

By now, the rest of the day staff had arrived. Kristen could hear their amiable chatter and laughter as she entered the conference room. She sat quietly and continued sipping her tea. During morning report, Kristen learned why Emma hadn't improved with the current antibiotics. "Emma has Legionnaire's?" she asked with disbelief.

"That's right," reported Rebecca, the charge nurse. "And unfortunately, she had a near-fatal allergic reaction to the most effective antibiotic. She's really between a rock and a hard place. Do you want to care for her again today?"

"Of course. Emma's been a delightful patient. I just hope there's a new antibiotic that she can take." Kristen tried to sound nonchalant, but felt a sudden lump in her throat along with a sense of foreboding.

"You know the risks. So just in case there isn't an antibiotic, don't get too close to her. The MICU is stressful enough without getting too emotionally involved with our patients," said Rebecca solemnly.

This is my usual load of patients, but somehow it seems endless. Kristen continued her morning trek from patient to patient, doing her usual nursing tasks, and saving Emma for last. After starting several intravenous lines, injecting multiple medications, dispensing seemingly countless pills, and doing other procedures, she finally donned the protective yellow gown and entered Emma's isolation room. Immediately she noticed Emma's still labored breathing, as she gently touched her hand.

"Sorry to awaken you, Emma, but I have your morning medications here."

Emma rubbed her eyes. "Oh my, was I asleep again? Seems like that's about all I do any more." She tried to raise herself up, but was too weak. "Guess you heard that I have Legionnaire's. No wonder the usual antibiotics haven't worked."

Kristen injected some medication into Emma's IV line. Knowing Emma was too weak to sit up, she elevated the head of her bed, and gave Emma her pills. After swallowing the pills, Emma studied Kristen's face. "I think something special happened to you recently."

"Nothing gets past you and those decades of living and nursing, does it?" responded Kristen.

"Not much," she chuckled.

Kristen sat on the edge of Emma's bed, and gently cradled her hand. " I didn't believe in angels or divine intervention until an incident occurred last night on the highway. Now I'm not sure what to believe. I should be dead or at least critically injured. There's just no logical explanation, except for divine intervention. I just don't understand why there was any intervention. Death is a common experience in every hospital. We see critically injured people of all ages all the time. And look at what you've been through!"

Emma turned towards Kristen. She studied her thoughtfully for a moment, and then gently responded, "I don't have all the answers. However, from my personal perspective, I've gained inner strength through my challenges that I would never have achieved otherwise. I truly believe God's promise to Joshua applies to all of us: 'Be strong and of a good courage; be not afraid, neither be thou dismayed: for the Lord thy God is with thee whithersoever thou goest.' That's in Joshua 1:9. However, God's admonition to Joshua is based on his obedience to God's commandments. And that applies to all of God's children."

Emma paused for a minute, while Kristen jotted the verse down. Then she went on, "Now both our lives have been spared through God's intervention. That is a humbling gift. Since my accident, my life long quest has been to search and fulfill God's purpose for me. It might sound preachy, but I believe that divine intervention should always be followed by a heart-felt choice that will change your life forever. That choice is to focus on three life-changing qualities: gratitude, introspection, and submission to God's will."

Kristen took a deep breath and closed her eyes for a moment, pondering Emma's words. "What you've said doesn't sound preachy, but it is so profound that I need time to absorb it. I've haven't thought about God's purpose for sparing my life. I don't know where to begin."

"Why don't you come back later when your shift is done and we'll talk. Would that be alright?"

"Absolutely!" responded Kristen with a smile.

Emma hesitated for a moment. "And sometime I'd like to share another personal story with you, but only when you're ready."

Kristen patted Emma's hand. "You've shared a lot with me already."

At the end of her shift, Kristen sat in the cramped computer area and typed the last of her notes on each patient. Being able to sit and rest after eight hours of non-stop nursing felt blissfully wonderful. With the completion of her last chart, Kristen began wondering again about her life-sparing experience from the night before. *"I wonder if Emma is right about me needing to learn why God intervened and what my purpose is on Earth. Guess I'll go see if she's awake."*

Rebecca saw Kristen getting ready to leave the computer room. "I'm finished now, too. Didn't have a chance for lunch so I'm going for a bite to eat. Care to join me? "

"Oh, no thanks. Not this time. I'm going to see Emma for a few minutes and then go home."

"How's she doing?"

Kristen took the stethoscope from around her neck and put it in her pocket as she thought about her answer. "Well, Dr. West talked to her about an experimental antibiotic and Emma consented to try it. I gave her the first dose this afternoon. I certainly hope that she starts improving over the next 24 hours. Right now she seems to be holding her own."

"That's good. But remember she's quite weak. Don't get your hopes up," cautioned Rebecca solemnly.

"I can't help it. She's been through so much. It wouldn't be fair for her to die now."

"Kristen, life isn't fair," replied Rebecca firmly.

She looked at Rebecca with astonishment. "Emma said the same thing."

"Well, Emma's right. And you already know that from being a critical care nurse."

"I have to believe that Emma will survive," she responded emphatically as she turned and walked towards Emma's room.

As always, Kristen donned the protective yellow gown before entering Emma's room. Emma was sipping some cranberry juice. Instinctively, Kristen checked her heart monitor, IV site for signs of infection, and then her oxygen level. Then her eyes met Emma's.

"Well you survived another day in the ICU. Please sit down and rest your weary body."

"You remember that weariness from ICU nursing?"

"Like it was yesterday." Emma laughed, and then began coughing. Kristen tried to suppress her growing concern.

When her coughing spell was over, Emma smiled and said, "Tell me about your day,"

Kristen sat slowly down in the chair by the bed and sighed, "I'm definitely worn out. However, in between the patients and the emergencies, I've thought some about what you said this morning. But how does anyone figure out what God wants them to do with their life, especially after His divine intervention saves them?"

"Well, Kristen, I'm not a theologian. I can only share what I've learned."

Kristen quickly responded, "I believe that you've learned well, because I feel such peace when I'm with you."

Emma bowed her head for a moment. Her blue eyes were glistening with tears as she gazed at Kristen's face. "Peace comes from choosing to submit to God. I always take time to pray every morning and every night before I go to bed. I didn't do this regularly before my accident, I guess because daily prayers didn't seem necessary. When I pray, I ask for guidance, and I've learned to allow time for the divine inspiration that I've asked for. Remember that God doesn't communicate with humankind through neon signs. I've learned to listen to His quiet promptings. I also developed the habit of scheduling time regularly for introspection—at least a couple of hours away from home and office, away from where I always feel compelled to work and answer the phone."

Kristen gazed intently at Emma, as though absorbing every word. Emma paused for a moment, and then asked, "Kristen, have you ever taken the time to write down what you want to achieve with your life?"

She hesitated. "It seems like a logical thing to do. But I'm sorry to say that I haven't."

"No need to be sorry. It's so easy to get caught up with the hustle and bustle of life that many—and possibly the majority—of people never get out of the rut they've created. And finally we're put in the permanent six by six by four foot cemetery plot. Unfortunately, the 'go-to-work and pay-the-bills' rut usually doesn't empower anyone to achieve their full potential, or fulfill their dreams. But we only get one life to live. Some of us are lucky enough to get a jolt to remind us of that fact. And remember that in the poorest areas of our world, people have to devote most of their time every day to scrounge up one meal for their family. So we're in a very fortunate group to begin with. Anyway Kristen, this is a suggestion of something I found helpful when needing to sort through things. On your way home, stop at a small restaurant so that you don't have to cook dinner, clean house or attend to the hundreds of tasks and distractions that consume our time at home or work. I've done this in quiet places like a park or the mountains, but it's rather cold for that right now. Remember to take a notebook with you. After some nourishment, take time to think about things you want to do in your life. You might want to consider categories such as family and friends, intellectual, physical, career, and most important of all, spiritual." Emma paused for a moment. "Think about the acronym NOVA, which is: Numerate your dream of achievement; Organize your specific goals; Visualize what you want; Act on it." Kristen took out her note book and quickly jotted down the NOVA acronym.

"NOVA. Isn't that a star that becomes brighter?"

"Yes. It becomes a thousand times brighter before it fades. We only have a certain amount of time to work on our dreams to make them a reality. I've founding life most rewarding when I've used those dreams to brighten our lives and others as well."

Kristen clasped her hands around Emma's. "Wow! That's truly awesome!"

Emma smiled weakly. "It helped me. When we visualize our goals, and let our subconscious minds work on those goals, we can tap into an amazing creative power. Kristen, also think about service. Although you serve your patients every day, I found some of the most gratifying experiences of my life were in performing acts of service, especially anonymous acts of service. I've even done some nursing in medically under-served countries, which was very demanding, but extremely rewarding. One of the most motivating teachings to me from Jesus is found in Matthew 25:35-40. Why don't you read it out loud for both of us?"

Emma opened her own bible to the verses in Matthew and handed the book to Kristen. And so she read for the first time: "For I was an hungred, and ye gave me meat; I was thirsty, and ye gave me drink; I was a stranger, and ye took me in; Naked, and ye clothed me; I was sick, and ye visited me; I was in prison, and ye came unto me. Then shall the righteous answer him, saying, Lord, when saw we thee an hungred, and fed thee? Or thirsty, and gave thee drink? When saw we thee a stranger, and took thee in? or naked, and clothed thee? Or when saw we thee sick, or in prison, and came unto thee? And the King shall answer and say unto them, Verily I say unto you, Inasmuch as ye have done it unto one of the least of these my brethren, ye have done it unto me."

Kristen paused for a moment and reflected. "Wow, those are

powerful scriptures."

"There's so many good works that need to be done in the world. If everyone would do some good to help those in need, the world would be so much better."

Kristen jotted down those scriptures to look up at home and then thought for a moment about what Emma had just said. "I didn't know that you worked in other countries. You're a remarkable woman!"

Before she could respond, Emma began coughing again. When the coughing had lessened, Kristen handed her a glass of juice. "Maybe I should go and you can finish tomorrow."

She sipped some juice and then continued. "No, please stay. I always want to finish what I've begun," she replied weakly.

After catching her breath, she proceeded. "Tonight after you finished writing your goals, go to a quiet place, such as a library or chapel, and prayerfully consider your list. See what else comes to mind. God usually has other goals in mind for His children. I always found it helpful to listen to the quiet inspiration that came to me. It was during one of those prayerful times of contemplation that I felt prompted to go to graduate school. Until then, I'd never thought about graduate school. However, that career change helped me to heal emotionally, challenged me intellectually, and allowed me to serve both patients as well as students."

"Considering what you've accomplished, that career change seems like a perfect choice."

Emma smiled. "It wasn't my choice initially. I had never even thought about graduate school material. But it felt like the right path, so I pursued it. Because I was accepted into graduate school, it seemed like I should continue to emphasize spiritual goals, such as praying daily, reading the scriptures daily, and especially living God's commandments." Emma let out a sigh and closed her eyes.

"I'm sorry, it looks like I've worn you out," said Kristen worriedly.

"Don't you worry. I was just thinking. Imagine what this world would be like if people chose to live just the Ten Commandments. You know that when God met Moses and gave him the two tablets of stone, they were engraved with the 'Ten Commandments' not the 'The Ten Suggestions'".

Kristen smiled at the ludicrous and incongruous thought. "Unfortunately the 'Ten Suggestions' is how much of the world regards them."

"But just imagine what the world would be like if people in general hadn't decided that God was old-fashioned and therefore wrong! Furthermore, God didn't put a time-limit on His commandments," Emma said with surprising intensity.

As Kristen mused over the ramifications of the entire world's population living the Ten Commandments, she nodded in agreement. "It would be an unbelievably peaceful world if people just followed those ten, simple commandments. The courts and jails wouldn't be burdened. Imagine our police, lawyers and judges being bored due to a lack of criminals! We wouldn't have to worry about our homes and businesses being robbed, or especially people being murdered."

Emma nodded her head in agreement. "That's certainly true. But there's even more than our legal standards for criminal behavior. Have you thought about how society and people suffer because of violation of the seventh commandment?"

"The seventh commandment?" Kristen thought for a few seconds. " Oh, the 'Scarlet Letter' commandment: 'Thou shalt not commit adultery.' Our society acts like the seventh commandment has been erased."

"It hasn't been erased! And actually, the scriptures make it clear that all forms of sexual immorality are wrong," responded Emma emphatically.

"If that includes premarital sexual relations, that's asking a lot in our society."

Emma tilted her head slightly and looked directly at Kristen. "I'm not asking it. It's been God's commandment since the beginning of humankind. Despite what the entertainment world has glamorized, and the lives that many of the idols as well as the leaders of our society have lived, violating that one commandment has created terrible ramifications for society. Just ponder for a moment on the tragic consequences that people suffer by violating God's standard of morality: unwed mothers, teenage pregnancies, abortions of unwanted children, fatherless children, broken marriages, terrible sexually transmitted diseases and even death, to name a few. There are also countless tragic emotional repercussions, as well as numerous crimes of passion."

Kristen nodded in agreement. "The consequences are truly abysmal. When I read the book "The Scarlet Letter" in high school, I was appalled at the punishment that poor woman was forced to endure. But there was no punishment for the man—after all, it takes two. In that case, it was the minister, who was never punished. And even now hundreds of years later, in the Middle East and other countries, it's only the women who are stoned death or even worse. And in the other extreme is the behavior in the Western World. The other night, I was watching a movie and afterwards I just felt so depressed by the current portrayal of romance, as though sex is a substitute for devotion to a life-long spouse. That's not what I envisioned true love to be."

Emma nodded in agreement. "You know, what we seldom hear about are the countless, devout and happily married couples who fully live that commandment as God defined it in the Bible. They are celibate until they are married, and thereafter have intimate relations only with each other."

"That's what my parents taught to my sister and me. It's certainly the way they chose to live," acknowledged Kristen.

Gazing out the window a couple of minutes, Emma then quietly continued, "I was engaged twice. The first time, my fiancé was in the Marines. He died serving in Vietnam."

She paused and took a sip of juice before resuming, "My second fiancé courted me 11 months before we were married. Then we were married for only a week when Henry was killed in an accident. Both deaths were tragic from our limited perspective, because two good men died in the prime of their lives."

Emma looked intently at Kristen and said emphatically, "I can't tell yet you why I know this, but, I absolutely understand what is important from God's eternal perspective. But from His perspective, the most important part of any couple's relationship is choosing to abide by His commandments, including celibacy. Following God's moral laws is so very crucial, Kristen. Couples who think that they can rationalize becoming intimate before marriage—no matter how well they live the other commandments—are, quite simply, wrong. God requires that we live all His commandments, not just those that are convenient or those that we agree with. After I married Henry, even though my honeymoon only lasted a week, I've never had any regrets about obeying the seventh commandment."

"But how did you control your passion for one another?" asked Kristen.

"First and foremost, my fiancés and I made that choice. That is to say, we chose to follow God's commandments about morality. Also, we chose to discuss this in the beginning of our relationship. But because the biological force between humans can be so strong, we also chose to take precautions, like avoiding movies with bedroom scenes, and limiting our passion to a simple goodnight kiss on the doorstep. Finally, we chose to focus on building an enduring friendship. We had so much fun together doing hobbies, like hiking. It was the same with my first fiancé, Josh before he was shipped out to serve in Vietnam. Henry also loved playing the guitar and singing for children. He'd take me with him to perform weekly at the Children's Hospital, even though I couldn't carry a tune in a bucket. By the time Henry were married, we knew each other very well and trusted one another completely. It's the best way to start a marriage." Emma opened her scriptures and retrieved a yellowed paper. "This is a poem about love that I learned when I was a teenager, which embodies what I believe true love is all about. I'd read it but I'm quite tired. Would you read it for me?"

Kristen gently held the yellowed paper and softly read:

I LOVE YOU

I love you not only for what you are,
but for what I am when I am with you.
I love you not only for what you have made of yourself,
but what you are making of me.
I love you because you have done more that any creed could have
done to make me good,
and more that any fate could have done to make me happy.
You have done it without a touch, without a word, without a sign.
You have done it my being yourself.

Perhaps that it what being a friend means after all.
Author Anonymous

Kristen felt a lump in her throat, and thought about the poem for a moment. "I can see what you mean. Perhaps this is another reason why I don't feel good about how much of our society treats romantic relationships. This is a beautiful poem, but I doubt that I'll ever find a man that I feel this way about love especially at my age."

"Much of life is unpredictable. But no matter what happens, just remember that God's love is always there, and to follow His Light."

"But people make all kinds of mistakes especially in the area of relationships. What happens to them?"

"You're right, because all of us are imperfect. But the most transcendent event of the world happened when Jesus Christ atoned for our sins. Remember the price he paid in Gethsemane when prayed to Heavenly Father. In Luke 22:44, the verse reads: 'And being in an agony he prayed more earnestly: and his sweat was as it were great drops of blood falling down to the ground.' Kristen, Christ's atoning sacrifice was for each of us. After Jesus was crucified, he was resurrected, proving that there truly was life after death. The Savior's atonement was the greatest act of His love to humankind. Jesus Christ paid the price for our sins, but that gift is based upon each of us repenting. Do you know what 'repent' means?"

"Not really."

Emma sipped some juice and then softly said, "To repent means to turn away from sin and to return to God. When we repent, we must confess our sins and ask for God's forgiveness. Then we must make restitution when possible and apologize to anyone who we offended. And finally we must change our lives to follow God." She closed her eyes for a moment, and then gazed out the window. Did you know that 'baptism' is from a Greek word meaning to 'dip' or 'immerse'?"

"No. That's interesting considering the variations in different religions and cultures."

"Actually baptism symbolizes death, burial and resurrection. It is clear that John the Baptist baptized in that manner, and he even baptized Jesus Christ that way. Read one last scripture, okay?"

Emma opened up her Bible to Matthew. "Read 3:13 through 17."

Kristen took the opened Bible and read the verses softly, "Then cometh Jesus from Galilee to Jordan unto John, to be baptized of him. But John forbad him, saying I have need to be baptized of thee, and comest thou to me? And Jesus answering said unto him, 'Suffer it to be so now: for thus it becometh us to fulfill all righteousness. Then he suffered him. And Jesus, when he was baptized, went up straightway out of the water; and, lo, the heavens were opened unto him, and he saw the Spirit of God descending like a dove, and lighting upon him; And lo a voice from heaven, saying 'This is my beloved Son, in whom I as well pleased."

"I think that is a beautiful account of Jesus Christ being baptized. The spirit of God descending like a dove was symbolic of the Holy Spirit, although John later stated that the Holy Spirit wouldn't be given until after Jesus was glorified, meaning resurrected. But the next verse is so clear about God the Father being pleased in His beloved Son, Jesus Christ." Emma sipped some juice and before concluding, "Peace on Earth. That's what we sing about this time of year. But we'll never experience true peace either individually or as a society unless we choose God. Choosing peace means choosing God. And choosing God means choosing righteousness by living His commandments. Our safety comes from repentance. Our strength comes from obedience to God."

Kristen gently clasped Emma's hand. "Thanks for sharing so much with me," she said with heartfelt kindness.

Emma placed her other hand on top of Kristen's. In a few minutes, she drifted off to sleep. Kristen quietly slipped out of her room. In the locker room, as she pulled on her wool slacks and sweater, she changed her plans for that night. On the way out of the hospital, Kristen stopped by the Christmas tree in the lobby. A few tags with names from an orphanage remained on the branches. Kristen remembered Emma's counsel on sharing love at Christmas and making good choices. *I need to make better choices in my life. This year I want to begin a tradition by making Christmas a more meaningful holiday by helping His children in need.* With a tag for a girl in her hand, she thought she was done. But Kristen felt compelled to also take the name for a boy. *I'll have to take some money out of savings or work an extra shift, but it will be worth it.*

Kristen tucked the names of the children into her pocket. In the frosty evening air, she stopped for a moment and gazed at the scenery. The mountains were capped with white snow, and had a rosy glow from the sun which was just beginning to set. The leafless trees no longer looked barren and lifeless. Instead, Kristen felt captivated by their beauty, with their branches outlined in glistening snow and pointed heavenward. Kristen found herself inexplicably gazing up. Then she surprised herself with her spontaneous, heartfelt prayer of gratitude: "Thanks, God, for letting me see this beauty. Guide me to know thy will for me. And thanks for Emma. She's taught me so much about life and about Thee. Please let her live."

Driving to a nearby store, she pondered what Emma had said. Inside, music blared overhead but it didn't drown the noise of the many shoppers. Kristen quickly walked to the music department and searched for the sacred music section. After glancing through a few CDs, she found what she was looking for and picked up several. *A couple for Emma and for my family and me,* she thought as she picked them up. She also gathered all her gifts for the two children at the orphanage, and then headed to the cashier. Back in the silence of her car, she opened one CD, slid it into the player, and listened joyfully to a choir singing Longfellow's, "I Heard the Bells on Christmas Day." As she drove into the parking lot of a small restaurant named Fernwood, she listened intently to the message of the last stanza:

"Till, ringing, singing, on its way, The world revolved from night to day, a voice, a chime, a chant sublime, Of peace on earth, good will to men!" *

Sighing contentedly, she found herself relaxing and rejoicing. *What a meaningful Christmas hymn!* Inside the restaurant, Kristen relaxed more as she gazed at the beautiful decor. The restaurant was decorated in natural tones with evergreen carpet. Several delicate ferns hung from the ceiling. In the small reception area was a Christmas tree, featuring ceramic angels, and cross-stitched ornaments with the message, "Peace Begins With Me." Enhancing the tranquil setting even further was the soft background music of

Christmas chimes ringing "I Heard the Bells on Christmas Day." *This is an interesting coincidence!*

The hostess returned from seating a couple. She saw Kristen standing by the Christmas tree, but picked up a pen and began writing. Kristen sighed and thought, *That's one of the reasons why I don't eat out often. It's like you don't exist when you're alone.*

"Excuse me, but I would like to be seated as well."

"Are you alone or are you waiting for someone?"

"I'm alone but I would still like to be seated." *I'm also waiting for someone, but I don't know his name, and I'm sure that he won't be here tonight,* Kristen thought sarcastically and then stopped herself.. *Alright, I'll work on not being cynical.*

The hostess looked surprised, but grabbed a menu and said curtly "Follow me please," as she quickly turned and led the way to a table for two by the kitchen door. *Okay, I'll just sit with my back to the kitchen door and pretend that this is the quietest table here.*

Kristen perused the menu, and selected the baked fish entree instead of her favorite of fried chicken. *I need to start eating healthier if I'm going to accomplish more goals.* She then took out her newly purchased notebook and divided the page into sections: Intellectual, Spiritual, Physical, Relationships, and Service. With Bach's "Jesu, Joy of Man's Desiring" playing softly in the background, Kristen began contemplating the goals that she wanted to achieve during the remainder of her life.

After dinner, Kristen stopped at her church where the choir happened to be rehearsing for their Christmas performance. Sitting in the quiet chapel, she remembered Emma's counsel about the divine intervention that saved her life on the highway the night before: "Choose gratitude, introspection, and submission to God's will." With a silent prayer, she reviewed her goals some more. As Emma had predicted, new goals came to Kristen's mind.

Returning home later than usual, she was greeted eagerly at the front door by Squeak. On the floor, lay one of her plants that had been knocked over. "Squeak, what am I going to do with you to keep you from knocking things over? I did leave some dry kitty food for you, which I now see that you haven't touched."

Squeak looked up innocently and softly meowed. Kristen

scooped some food into Squeak's dish, which was eagerly consumed. Quickly finished with her meal, she looked up and meowed contentedly "Squeak, I've never put up my mother's ceramic nativity scene before, but I really want to do that tonight. And you must try to refrain from knocking it over, okay?"

Kristen began playing her Christmas music, to continue the reflective mood. In her bedroom, she knelt down, reached under her bed, and pulled out a large box. Removing a layer of dust, she carefully carried it to the living room, with Squeak prancing excitedly beside her. On her antique, walnut corner table, she spread the white angel-hair. She attentively unwrapped each white ceramic figurine and placed them on the angel-hair. In the foreground were Mary, Joseph, and the baby Jesus in his cradle. Around them, Kristen placed several white ceramic shepherds and angels, as well as the three wise men. Then she took out a string of tiny white Christmas lights and delicately placed them around the edge of the table.. She sat on the floor and gazed at the nativity scene, feeling an unexpected sereneness. Squeak sat quietly next to her, with her tail gently swishing across the carpet. "This nativity scene and the Christmas hymns create such a quiescent and peaceful atmosphere. Even you're quiet, Squeak."

Kristen began her next project of wrapping Christmas presents. Bringing all the presents out, she arranged them by the fireplace. Squeak began her usual racing around the room, climbing into the large potted plant, and dashing over the sofa. Kristen tried to keep her from the nativity scene, but eventually gave up. Retreating to the bedroom, she returned with Christmas paper, tape and scissors. Her kitten had seemingly disappeared. Then to Kristen's amazement, she found Squeak lying quietly on the walnut table, behind the ceramic figures of Mary, Joseph, and the cradle holding the baby Jesus. Not a single ceramic figurine had been knocked down. She stared with disbelief. "Squeak, you're unbelievable. How did you manage to get to where you are without knocking over anything? It's like you know that you're on sacred ground."

Squeak looked at her, flicked her tail, and purred. It was too blissful of a scene to pass up. "Please, don't move an inch! Stay, stay right there." She quickly retrieved her camera, and took a picture.

"Without this picture, no one would believe that my impetuous kitten could actually do this without knocking anything over."

Squeak laid her head on her paws, curled her tail around her paws to her nose, closed her eyes and snoozed. As her kitten slept, Kristen continued listening to Christmas hymns and finished wrapping the presents.

*I Head the Bells on Christmas Day

I head the bells on Christmas Day, Their old familiar carols play,
And wild and sweet the words repeat, Of peace on earth,
good will to men.
I thought how as the day had come, The belfries of all Christendom
had rolled along the unbroken song, Of peace on earth,
good will to men.
And in despair I bowed my head: "There is no peace on earth,"
I said, "For hate is strong and mocks the song, Of peace on earth,
good will to men."
Then pealed the bells more loud and deep: "God is not dead, nor
doth he sleep, The wrong shall fail, the right prevail,
With peace on earth, good will to men."
Till, ringing, singing, on its way, The word revolved from night
to day, A voice, a chime, a chant sublime, Of peace on earth,
good will to men!

(Text: Henry Wadsworth Longfellow, 1807-1882; Music:
John Baptiste Calkin, 1827-1905)

Chapter Four

"Do Your Best, and Trust in God for the Rest."

The shrill ringing of her alarm abruptly ended Kristen's dreaming. In the dark, she blindly reached out to shut off the noise, but instead knocked both the clock and lamp off her bedside table. Down on her knees, she groped in the darkness of the early morning until she finally found the clock and turned off the incessant alarm. Then she found her lamp and fumbled for the switch. Squinting from the light, she felt her way to the bathroom. After splashing some cold water on her face and brushing her hair, she began to feel more awake. Enveloping herself in a fuzzy ivory robe, she turned up the thermostat on her way to her kitchen. Squeak, ravenous as usual in the morning, kept loudly meowing while curling herself around Kristen's leg. As quickly as possible, Kristen scooped out some kitty food into Squeak's dish. Then she poured some orange juice to raise her own blood sugar and to help her awaken, while toasting a piece of multigrain bread. With her toast and juice, Kristen made her way to the living room, where she turned on her CD player and the gas-log fireplace. As "Oh Come All Ye Faithful" was playing in the background, she nestled herself into a corner of her sofa. Squeak jumped up on the sofa as well, and curled up on her lap.

Opening up her notebook, Kristen thoughtfully studied the list of her goals that she had written the night before. "Squeak, I came up with more goals than I ever thought possible on my own. I've done a lot of hiking and repelling off cliffs, but never thought about preparing to climb Mount McKinley. Wow, that sounds like a great challenge! And just like Emma said, even more goals came to mind when I stopped in the chapel and prayed for guidance. I also never thought about going to graduate school and becoming a nurse practitioner, but I honestly feel that God is guiding me to that path, as well as doing service in medically under-served areas."

Kristen sighed as she stroked Squeak, who purred contentedly. "Wow, these goals seem awesome and overwhelming! I can't wait to share them with Emma—"

Jumping up abruptly, she scooped up Squeak and dashed to the phone. "Dear God, please let Emma be better," Kristen pleaded as she hastily dialed the number to the MICU. One of the night clerks answered.

"Hi. This is Kristen Matthews. I just need to know how Emma is doing."

"Kristen, aren't you coming in today?"

"Yes, but I couldn't wait. Please, just tell me how Emma is."

"Just a moment. I'll have you talk with one of the nurses."

The wait seemed interminable. *Why is this taking so long? I hope—.* She stopped herself from thinking the seemingly unthinkable, and clutched Squeak tighter.

"Kristen, this is Esther. What's up?"

"I just want to know how Emma is doing."

"Oh. Well, I haven't been caring for her. Let me check the computer. Well, let's see. Her vital signs are relatively stable, but her heart beat is still irregular. And she has a fever of 104 degrees. Anything else you want to know?"

"No, that's enough. Thanks." She sighed with relief.

"You're worrying too much. It's not healthy, as you know."

"I know, but Emma has become so special to me. Sorry to bother you. I'll see you in awhile."

Hurriedly she dressed while watching the morning news. She grabbed a granola bar and an apple to eat later. Stroking her kitten momentarily at the front door, she gently spoke, "Now here's a new toy to play with, along with your other toys. Please try to break anything while I'm gone."

Walking in the freezing cold to her car, Kristen silently added another goal to her list: *A house with an attached garage! It always seemed like I should wait until I was married to have a house. But I'm ready to move on with my life and have a home of my own, complete with a garage and yard and gardens.*

On her way to the hospital, Kristen hummed as she listened to the memorable Vienna Boys' Choir singing, "Little Drummer Boy." She felt a distinctive peace and calmness as she drove. Unexpectedly, a driver abruptly darted in front of her and suddenly braked, nearly causing an accident. Instead of her usual cursing, Kristen immediately recalled *"Okay, he's just a work in progress— hopefully."* And then she sang along with the choir. As she drove into the parking lot, the choir just finished singing, "Oh Little Town of Bethlehem." Walking through the parking lot, Kristen kept humming the last hymn, feeling a sense of goodwill. *This is a much, much better way to start the day,* she thought as she changed into her scrubs.

In Emma's room, Kristen quietly left the Christmas music CD, along with a player on her bedside table. *I'm sure that Emma will enjoy hearing "I Heard the Bells on Christmas Day", as well as the other Christmas hymns. And the music will also be a great distraction from the usual commotion here in the MICU.*

During morning report, Kristen munched on her apple, tapped her foot against the floor and doodled. She was disappointed but not surprised when Rebecca assigned Emma to another nurse. The day was intense because of admitting four critically ill patients and responding to two cardiac arrests. It wasn't until the end of her shift, that she had a chance to visit with Emma.

As she entered her room, she saw Emma still laboring to breath, and her temperature was still 104 degrees. Emma's eyes were closed, but her face radiated joy as she listened to the Christmas music and tapped her index finger to the rhythm on her bed. Kristen sat down on the edge of her bed.

Emma's eyes immediately opened and she cheerfully said, "Oh, my dear Kristen, thank you for the music! It's been wonderful!"

"It's the least that I could do with all the help you've been to me," she responded with a smile.

"I haven't really done anything. Just shared some of my life's lessons. Did you work on your goals last night?"

"Yes, and I'm so excited!"

"Just remember that if you have any goals like climbing Mount McKinley or doing nursing in under-served areas, you should start now because some of life's challenges might include problems beyond your control."

Kristen was shocked. "But how did you know? Those are two of my goals!"

Emma smiled. "I think we have a lot of things about our lives in common. I learned after my accident, which made it impossible to continue working as a life flight nurse that I had to be flexible in my goals. However, everyone should always have inspiring aspirations because they are the essence of a fulfilling life."

She nodded with understanding. "I didn't realize how inspiring goals were until last night when I began my list of lifetime goals."

"There's another goal that you probably didn't write down, because you couldn't bring yourself to write it."

Tears began to well up in her eyes. Emma gently touched Kristen's hand. "Go ahead and just say it."

"I've always wanted to be married and have a family," Kristen whispered. It was as though vocalizing the deepest yearning of her heart opened up years of broken dreams.

Emma softly stroked her hand and gently said, "I very much wanted to have children, too. Being married for only one week was not long enough for me to get pregnant. As I've shared, first losing my fiancé in combat and then losing my husband in an accident right after our honeymoon caused a black cloud of pain. But both experiences turned into intense spiritual journeys that changed my life for the better. Sometimes, we just have to trust in God."

"But—"

Emma put her finger to Kristen's lips, and quietly said, "Just do your best and then trust in God for the rest."

Kristen brushed away a tear, and responded wryly, "I'm not convinced. 'Do your best and trust in God for the rest' sounds too simplistic."

Emma began coughing, and then sipped some apple juice,

before answering. "It is simplistic—except for the power of God that exceeds our understanding. An equally important lesson is to learn a fundamental lesson from the 'What if 'questions. Those questions can haunt you and destroy you."

"What if?"

"Yes. After any negative event, most people ask themselves, 'What if I'd done this differently? 'What if I'd done that differently?' It's quite essential for each one of us to understand that we can't change the past. However, it's also crucial to remember that we can learn from events in our lives. After my husband's death, I wondered 'What if I had been driving instead of him?' But then I realized that I would never want him to endure the physical pain from the accident and surgeries, or the psychological pain that I had experienced. For awhile, I despised drunk drivers. However, my life became enriched when I visualized our roads being safer without drunk drivers, and then channeled my energy into dealing with the problems of alcoholism. It's so important that we learn from the past, prepare for the future, and live for the present."

"That does make a lot of sense," Kristen replied with a sigh.

Emma began coughing again. "I should go and let you rest," said Kristen.

"In awhile." She sipped some juice and then continued, "I'll be okay. But I want you to remember that our lives on earth are very short compared to eternity. I know that there are more single women than men. Maybe you won't ever marry. And women do have biological time clocks. But being single can be a gift, because it allows you the opportunity to follow other goals, like being a nurse in areas where your husband would be afraid for you to go. I'm sure that my husband wouldn't have been able to cope with me going to some of the places I went to as a nurse. But things change, and maybe you will meet your soul-mate. The most important thing for all of us is to live righteously. Pray for God's guidance in your plans for your future. And trust in God." She turned to the window and became pensive.

"What's wrong?"

"Oh, nothing's wrong. I just think it's time to impart something else with you. I shared with you my experience with the crash that killed my husband, and the message: 'Life isn't fair, but God's love is always there.' Now I think you're ready to hear about an even more miraculous experience. Remember I told you that I had cancer?"

She nodded. "Of course."

"Well, that occurred a few years ago. I hadn't been feeling well, but I was busy with my career, and chose to ignore my symptoms. When I felt too sick to even go to my office, I made an appointment to see my doctor. She felt an abdominal mass and got an ultrasound the same day, which revealed a large ovarian tumor. She arranged for surgery the next day with a gynecologist. However, during the operation, the gynecologist found that the cancer had already metastasized. He could see that cancer had spread to my colon and even my liver. He and the other surgeon considered my case to be hopeless. They just sutured the incision and told my widowed 85 year-old mother that I'd die within two weeks. That was shocking news to my mother. Equally distressing was my post-operative coma. But my mother wasn't ready for me to die, so she kept me on life-support." Emma's voice became a whisper. "When I regained consciousness four days later, I knew that I had gone through a life-after-death experience."

Too captivated to even respond, Kristen waited silently for Emma to proceed. The sounds of the MICU—beeps from monitors, conversations, pagers—were seemingly silenced. It was like a transcendent hush miraculously took place in the MICU. After a moment, Emma quietly explained. "I went through a tunnel of light, similar to what others have described in life-after-death books. But that tunnel is truly indescribable. Afterwards, I saw deceased relatives, including my father, and my baby brother who died a few hours after his birth. Seeing my baby brother was a shock because we'd been taught in our religion that babies who died before being blessed wouldn't go to heaven. There was such a pervasive feeling of purity, love, peace and joy in that glorious place. It was overwhelming." She lay motionless, with tears gently cascading down her pale cheeks. "I wanted to stay. But I was told that my time on earth wasn't yet completed, and there was more for me to do. When I regained consciousness a few days later, I told my mother about my amazing experiences. She didn't know what to think. First of all, she'd been told by the surgeons that I'd be dead in a few days. And secondly, she was thrilled that I had seen my father and baby brother. Anyway, my doctors decided that since I'd survived the two weeks, they should give me chemotherapy. Chemo was rough, of course, but I knew God wanted me to endure because it just wasn't my time to die."

Kristen was totally enthralled with Emma's account. At a loss for words, she reached out and lovingly squeezed Emma's hand.

Emma continued in a gentle but intense tone. "This experience is why I can say with absolute certainty what God expects from us. Now, there are some extremely important things that I want you to know. One is that God loves us, but eternal law requires obedience to His commandments. To experience true joy, we must choose to obey His commandments. And because none of us know when we will die, we must use our time wisely. God understands that we aren't perfect, but He wants us to turn to Him, repent of our sins, overcome our faults, and strive to live righteously. We should pray for His guidance in living each day righteously and fully. God will help each of His children to become better. Secondly, remember that families are very important. Gifts can't replace your time, kindness and love. Those who don't have spouses or children, usually have grandparents, parents, siblings, aunts and uncles or cousins. Show your family your love, not just at Christmas but all year long. Remember that the best gift you can give someone is to be with them, especially during times of need. Hearts entwined together in love can endure much. Thirdly, we must also share that love with those in need, including the homeless, those in the hospital and so forth."

Emma looked out her window pensively for a moment, before turning back. "Finally, remember that even though life isn't fair, God's love is always there. When you're lonely, discouraged or sad, you must remember to pray for His peace. God's sublime and exquisite peace surpasses all understanding."

Kristen felt consumed by the warmth of God's power and presence. In her heart of hearts, she knew that what Emma had said was true. She searched for the right words but it was awhile before she could speak. "Thanks for sharing that incredible experience with me. And that's the most eloquent sermon I've ever felt!"

Emma smiled weakly. "Tomorrow is Christmas. There's no greater gift than we can give to Christ to celebrate His birthday than committing ourselves to greater righteousness. It's been a tradition of mine each December to make a resolution to God about some improvement in my life. I write at least one goal down on a card, place the card in a small box, and wrap the present in gold paper. That's the first part of NOVA. Do you remember the rest?"

"Of course," she responded with a grin. Numerate your dream of achievement. Organize your specific goals. Visualize those goals. Act on them."

"You're doing very well. Now, do you know why I choose gold paper each year to wrap my present to Jesus?"

"Well, I'm guessing that it symbolizes one of the three gifts from the wise men who sought the Christ-child to worship Him."

"Right. Those gifts were: gold, frankincense, and myrrh. Just something to think about on Christmas Eve. Now you had better go. I'm sure that you have lots to do."

"I don't want to leave, but you're right. I already had plenty to do, and now, after listening to you, I have even more! Anything you need before I go?"

"A little hug would be nice."

She smiled as she bent down and gently hugged Emma. "Thank you for everything."

Kristen stopped at the computer area by the nurses' station to make sure that her charting was completed. As she was perusing her last chart, Dr. Bennett sat down and began typing in a chart. Remembering her promise to Anna, Kristen decided to try the 'sandwich technique' that Emma had taught her.

"You know, Dr. Bennett, I've been very impressed with your ability and willingness to answer the numerous questions of the interns and students."

"You have?" he asked with a tone of surprise.

"Well, yes. You're a great teacher, except—" She hesitated as her anxiety grew.

Dr. Bennett scowled. "Except what?" he demanded.

Taking a deep breath, she plunged ahead. "Well, except, that after being the leader for a cardiac arrest, it's a good idea to express some appreciation to the team for their endeavors. It's a team effort you know. And it's not often that we have a successful resuscitation."

"And I suppose I shouldn't yell at a nurse for dropping anything?" he asked rather sarcastically.

This isn't going too well. Now what? wondered Kristen, with her gut twisting into knots.

But Dr. Bennett continued in a softer voice, "Between you and me, I get so stressed with cardiac arrests, because I hate for patients to die. Since childhood, I wanted to be a doctor, but I wanted to heal people, not see them die before my eyes. I feel like an absolute failure in the face of death."

So it's fear behind the facade of arrogance! And then Kristen remembered another lesson from Emma. Without hesitation she quietly repeated her simple phrase: "Just do your best, and then trust in God for the rest."

Immediately, she regretted her words, not knowing if he even believed in God.

Dr. Bennett rubbed his neck. "Do your best and trust in God. That's terribly simplistic. But you're right. That's all anyone can do. I'll work on the 'trusting in God' part. Of course, it would probably help if I attended church more regularly."

Kristen was surprised and pleased with his response. Then she recalled the remainder of the 'sandwich technique'. "I just want you to also remember that we enjoy working with you. You're an excellent physician and teacher."

"Well, thanks. I'll try to do better at praising the staff. You're really a great bunch of nurses."

"That would be greatly appreciated," she said with a feeling of relief. "By the way, you're not 'on call' tonight, are you?"

"No. I just needed to finish this chart and then planned on some studying."

"You know that medicine is endless. Please go home and spend some time with your family. They are the most precious people to you on earth. They need your time and love, especially on Christmas Eve."

Dr. Bennett looked surprised. "It's Christmas Eve? I'd forgotten. Working here 80 or more hours a week here puts you in kind of a time-warp."

He quickly logged off the computer and pushed himself away from the desk. "Alright. Let's get out of here."

At the women's locker room, their paths separated. As Dr. Bennett continued walking down the hallway, he waved to Kristen and cheerfully cried out, "Merry Christmas."

Kristen waved back in wonderment at the transformation before her eyes. She joyfully said "Merry Christmas!" And to herself she thought, *Looks like that 'work in progress' is progressing nicely.*

As she changed from her scrub suit into her winter clothes, Kristen decided to visit her Uncle Earl's home. *I've neglected visiting him because it's so difficult to see him wasting away. If only he had quit smoking years ago.*

The sun was approaching the horizon when she stopped by a grocery store and picked up some of Earl's favorite foods. Several other people were doing their last minute shopping before the stores closed. At Earl's home, Kristen shivered in the cold on the front porch after ringing the doorbell. In a moment, her Aunt Bessie answered the door. "Kristen, what a nice surprise!"

"Merry Christmas!" Kristen smiled as she hugged Bessie and tried to ignore the smell of tobacco. *The socially acceptable weapon that causes so much misery and suffering, including my parent's premature deaths.*

She followed Bessie into the living room where Earl was sitting in his recliner by the fireplace watching television. Earl's gaunt face lit up and he smiled when he saw her.

"Kristen, it's so good to see you. Did you just get off work?" asked Earl.

"Yes. Thought I'd drop by to share some eggnog and fruitcake with you and Bessie."

"How wonderful! My favorite holiday treats! It's been awhile since we've seen you."

"I'm sorry for being so neglectful," she said as she took off her parka.

"Don't you fret about that. I know you're busy with your work. Besides you see enough sickness every day."

Bessie returned with some glasses and began pouring the pale yellow egg nog. Raising their glasses together, Earl said cheerfully, "Merry Christmas!"

They visited amiably as they nibbled on fruit cake and sipped egg nog. "Kristen, I don't know if you have plans for tonight, but we would love to have you join us for dinner, if you have the time," invited Earl.

She wavered for a moment because there was so much left to do. Then Emma's words came to her forcefully, "Love your family." *And this will certainly be the last Christmas Earl has on earth.*

"Of course, I'd love to. Let me just call my sister."

In the kitchen, the aroma of the roast caused her mouth to water as she called her sister's number. "Hello, Kathryn. I decided to stop at Earl and Bessie's home. And they've invited me to stay for dinner. You'll forgive me if I don't join you tonight?"

"We'll miss you, but I understand. How's Uncle Earl doing?"

"Well right now he's enjoying his eggnog."

"Remind them that we'll be over to see both of them tomorrow. And then we'll see you when you get off work, okay?"

"Sure. Merry Christmas, Kathryn, and—" she paused for a second. "I love you."

"Well, Merry Christmas to you. And I love you. You're a great sister!"

Well maybe not a great sister. I'm pretty neglectful. But I'll try harder.

While she was talking with her sister, Bessie had set an extra place at the table and sliced the roast. Earl slowly made his way to the kitchen table. As Kristen hung up the phone, she turned and saw Earl leaning against a kitchen chair. She was shocked to see how thin he was. They sat down together, and Earl offered thanks to God for their dinner.

It was late by the time Kristen left Earl and Bessie's home. At her own home, she found Squeak ensconced in the ceramic nativity scene. Her kitten walked delicately among the ceramic figures to the edge of the table, stretched and jumped off. Scampering to the kitchen, she rubbed her back against Kristen's leg, as some kitty food was scooped into her dish. Squeak ate ravenously. "Sorry, I'm late, Squeak. I just had to spend some time with my Uncle Earl and Aunt Bessie." Kristen stroked Squeak, as her tail waved rhythmically.

In the living room, Kristen started listening to the Mormon Tabernacle Choir singing Handel's "Messiah". There were already several presents wrapped and stacked by the fireplace. But there were more presents to wrap. And after hearing Emma's saga, she'd decided to add a few special gifts from her heart. Her heart filled with joy as she listened to the Hallelujah chorus. Her last gift was a hand-written card which she put in a small box. She carefully wrapped the box in gold paper, and labeled the card, "To: Jesus. Love, Kristen."

Chapter Five

The Secret of Christmas Gladness

Despite getting to bed around midnight, when Kristen's alarm rang, she awakened quickly. Stretching, she exclaimed joyfully out loud, "Merry Christmas!" Squeak jumped on the bed, and licked her chin. She gave her kitten a hug, and then carried her to the living room. Flicking the switch to her fireplace, the room was filled with a warm glow. By the antique walnut table, she knelt and turned on the tiny lights surrounding the serene nativity scene. "What a beautiful reminder of this extraordinary celebration," she said quietly while stroking her Squeak who was snuggled beside her.

With Christmas music in the background, she quickly dressed. While she was braiding her hair, Squeak played with her fuzzy slippers. As "Joy to the World, the Lord has Come" was sung, Kristen sang along with elation. When the hymn was finished, she noticed Squeak watching her intently. "Squeak, this is a glorious day when we celebrate the birth of our Savior," she explained while stroking under her chin.

Turning the television onto the morning news, she sipped some orange juice, while her oatmeal cooked. "My forecast for a white Christmas came true!" the weatherman announced cheerily. "We received another six inches last night. Bad news for the people who must drive to work this morning, but great news for the rest! And here is some more good news: the storm has passed and it's going to be a sunny and cloudless day."

Kristen bundled up in her winter coat, gloves and boots. She made two trips to her car in the cold darkness of the early morning carrying the sacks of gifts for her family and for co-workers. *I'm definitely getting a house with an attached garage!*

On her last trip out of her home, she hugged Squeak and pulled a red ball with a bell inside it. "Here's a new toy just for you. Now, be good and I'll see you later." Quickly engrossed with the ball, Squeak began batting it around the sofa causing a lively ringing that filled the room. Kristen quickly shut the front door while Squeak was distracted.

The snow plows had already cleared the highway, which was virtually empty, making the commute easier than usual following a storm. Kristen listened with joyful rapture to Christmas hymns by Placido Domingo. She also thought about the impulsive gifts and notes she had done the night before for the MICU staff. *I hope that my co-workers don't think my gifts and notes are too corny.*

In the parking lot, she glanced at her watch. *Good—it's only 6:30, so I should be ahead of the rest of the staff.* In the moonlight and parking lot lights, the new snow glistened like a field of countless crystals. Carefully carrying her sack of gifts across the snow-covered parking lot, she entered the hospital, stomped the snow off her boots, and jogged up the stairs to the fourth floor. While dressing, she recalled Placido Domingo majestically singing "O, Holy Night." The words brought solace to her heart as she thought about the suffering of Uncle Earl, Emma, and all the other patients.

Kristen took her sacks of gifts to the MICU. In the mail boxes, she placed decorated containers of nuts and dried fruits for her co-workers. *I'm certainly glad that I bought that dehydrator and began drying fruits last summer!* To each gift was attached a brief personalized note of appreciation.

Emma was sleeping soundly. But her labored breathing and fever persisted. *I'm afraid that the new antibiotic isn't helping her.* Kristen looked out the window and up at the starry sky. *God, please don't let Emma die. She's been through so much.* And then she remembered, Emma's counsel: "Do your best, and trust in God for the rest."

It was seven o'clock and time for staff meeting. Reluctantly, Kristen left Emma's bedside, leaving another CD of Christmas hymns on her bedside table. Rebecca saw her leaving Emma's room. She gently put her arm around Kristen's shoulders as they walked to the conference room. "There's some bad news about Emma. She had a chest x-ray yesterday that showed pleural fluid, so the resident sent some fluid for analysis. That analysis came back late yesterday. It shows cancer cells."

Kristen groaned and shook her head. "She didn't tell me about that when I spoke with her yesterday. So she's got lung cancer as well. I guess that's also why she's not getting better."

"Her doctors suspect it's a recurrence of her ovarian cancer that's spread to her lungs. Do you still want to take care of Emma today?"

"Absolutely!"

"Okay. I trust you'll find a way to handle whatever happening."

"I will," she said with more conviction than she felt.

The rest of the staff was seated around the table, munching on the nuts and dried fruit and reading the notes Kristen had given them. There was a ripple of "Thanks" from the nurses.

Sipping some orange spice tea, Kristen tried to put into words her feelings. "Well, I've worked with most of you for several years. I just wanted you to know how much I appreciate each one of you."

Patrick grinned at Kristen. "Thanks also for the Hanukkah card, even though we celebrated that religious holiday earlier this month!"

"I'll work on that next year," she responded, forcing a smile, while trying to not worry about Emma.

"Merry Christmas!" cheerfully announced Esther, the charge nurse for the night shift, as she entered the conference room. "Now, if you don't mind, I'd like to get this report over so I can go home to my family." Quiet descended, and Esther reported on each patient, as the rest of the staff jotted notes on their patients.

Emma slept most of the day. At the end of her shift, Kristen found Emma awake and listening to the Christmas hymns. She was also smiling. "You look happy, no matter how you feel," she said as she sat on the edge of her bed.

Emma smiled and patted Kristen's hand. "And that's a result of—"

"An attitude of gratitude." Kristen responded feeling torn between sadness over Emma's health, but also joy for the lessons she had learned.

"I'm glad that you remembered. I know that to grow in life, we need challenges. Every day, I thank God for my blessings—even today. When I've faced trials, I've found them to also be opportunities for inner growth. His divine guidance and comfort has been a great solace especially now. He will do the same for you. Just seek God."

"How can you feel happy knowing that you've got a recurrence of your cancer?"

"Because God extended my life once and now I know that I've completed what God wanted me to do." Emma reached for her Bible, and retrieved a folded piece of paper. "This is something I wrote years ago when I was recovering from my accident. It's not Shakespeare, but it reflects my feelings about Christmas. Would you please read it out loud?"

Kristen unfolded the yellowed paper, and softly read the poem:

<u>The Secret of Christmas Gladness</u>
The secret of Christmas gladness,
Comes from touching hearts with kindness,
For people far and near,
Not just on Christmas day, but throughout the year.

The secret of Christmas gladness,
Comes from filling your soul with goodness,
By thanking God who sent His Son from above,
and by sharing Christ's light and love.

"That is a meaningful poem. I'd like to copy it," said Kristen.

Emma began coughing again. When the coughing spell ended, she saw the look of worry on Kristen's face. She held Kristen's hand. "Don't worry about me. Please take the poem with you. Now go and spend the rest of Christmas day with your sister and her family. Share your love with them. They are your family."

She gave a gentle hug to Emma. "Merry Christmas." And then a phrase came to her that she had never spoken before. "Godspeed, Emma." Reluctantly, she walked to the door. Emma waved, and then closed her eyes as she began listening to the Christmas music once again.

Outside, Kristen was momentarily captivated by the beauty of the day. The cloudless blue sky that the weatherman had promised was accurate. The pure white snow glistened brilliantly in the sunshine. As she gazed up into the azure sky, she recalled Emma's words: "An attitude of gratitude." She felt moved to utter a quiet prayer: "Thanks, God, for letting me see so much, including the beauty of this Christmas day. I also thank Thee for Emma, and for what she has taught me. Help me to remember Thee during my challenging times. And please be with Emma."

Kristen stopped at her home briefly to pick up the dinner rolls and her kitten. "Merry Christmas, Squeak. Can't leave you at home by yourself, while the family is celebrating Christmas." Kristen carefully tucked Squeak inside her parka, shielding her from the cold. In the car, she enticed Squeak into the kitty carrier by placing some treats inside it. Squeak quickly crawled inside, ate the treats, and settled down for a nap on a warm blanket.

The highway was surprisingly busy with cars filled with families. However, no one was speeding, or weaving from lane to lane, or cutting others off. *"The streets would certainly be much safer if people would drive as reasonably as this every day!"*

At Kathryn's home, Kristen began to take her sacks of gifts out of her car trunk. Cydney, her 16-year old niece, ran outside and gave her a hug. "Merry Christmas, Aunt Kristen!"

"And Merry Christmas to you, Cydney! Would you please carry a sack?"

"Sure. Mom said that you're bringing the turkey. Did you remember?"

"What? A turkey? But—"

Cydney grinned as she interjected. "Just kidding! We all knew that you were at work."

"Good, because all I brought is some dinner rolls."

Inside the two-story home, there was a buzz of activity. Kristen's nephew, Brent, was in the living room guarding the tree from his two toddlers who were giggling and playing with their new toys. "Merry Christmas, Aunt Kristen!" greeted Brent with a grin and a hug. "You're lucky that you weren't any later because the turkey just finished cooking, and you know this crowd wouldn't wait for long for anyone!"

"Thanks for the warning. And Merry Christmas to you, too. Where's your wife?"

"Melanie's helping Mom and Dad in the kitchen."

She removed her coat, while Squeak climbed out of the kitty carrier. Her kitten immediately began batting around a ball with the family cat.

Dave emerged from the kitchen and hugged Kristen. "He's right about this crowd and food, you know! Come into the kitchen where the real action is! I'm just getting ready to carve the turkey. Oh, and Merry Christmas."

"And Merry Christmas to you, Dave. How's my number one brother-in-law?"

"Great. I love the distinction of being your number one brother-in-law, even though the field is pretty narrow because you have only one sister!"

Dave guided her into their bright, spacious kitchen with its vaulted ceiling and skylight. She glanced up at the rays of sunlight shimmering through the skylight. *And I want a home with a kitchen larger than my dinky one that three people can barely squeeze into! And lots of windows so that I can actually grow plants!*

Strains of Christmas music from the stereo in the family room added to the cheer. Brent's wife, Melanie, was stirring the gravy on the stove. Kristen put her arm around her shoulders. "Merry Christmas, Melanie."

Melanie wrapped her free arm around her and hugged her. "And Merry Christmas to you, too."

Kristen greeted her sister, Kathryn, with a hug. "Merry Christmas."

"And Merry Christmas to you! You look a bit worn out. Hope your shift in the ICU wasn't too difficult."

THE CHRISTMAS MESSENGER

Kristen was trying hard to not think about Emma, even though she knew that Emma would tell her that all was well and to focus on her family. "It's been a little rough, but now it's time now to just focus on my family. So, anything I can do to help?"

Kathryn looked around. "Well, okay, Sis. How about putting the food on the table?"

Kristen picked up the vegetable casserole and walked to the large table in the dining room covered with a white linen table cloth that was decorated with red poinsettias. Seth, her nephew, was pouring cranberry juice into the goblets. "Merry Christmas, Seth! How's college going?"

Seth, at six feet and two inches tall, was the tallest man in the family. "Fine, but I'm sure glad that semester finals are over."

"So have you figured out what you want to be when you grow up, after your first semester? That's usually a perpetual question among college students, and even later in life."

Seth grimaced. "Not really. I'm still thinking about astronomy. You know that I've been captivated by astronomy ever since I first looked through a telescope when I was twelve. But my roommate is pre-med. He and you keep me interested in medicine."

Dave entered the dining room with the sliced turkey. "Notice that my youngest son didn't say anything about architecture—the love of my life?"

"That's nothing to fret about. Besides, it's always helpful to have a doctor in the family."

"Right. Well, when are you going to let me design a home for you?" asked Dave.

Kathryn brought in the salad, followed by Melanie with the mashed potatoes and gravy. "Now, Dave, you have good intentions, but Kristen has to make up her own mind. So let's eat."

Dave persisted. "I just don't know how you can stand that dark apartment. There's so little light that you can't even grow philodendrons! I did okay on our home, didn't I? Wouldn't you enjoy a home like ours?"

Kristen glanced around the dining room and into the family room. She thought for a moment before responding. *I definitely want a home, but I have too much on my mind right now to get started.*

I think that I'd better hold off telling them about my intentions for a while. Then she faced her brother-in-law: "Dave, you designed a gorgeous home for yourself and your family. But I don't need four bedrooms, a guest room, living room, family room, exercise room, and den."

"But things change. You might get mar—"

Dave was cut off from completing his sentence by his wife with one of those looks that couples share. "I think it's time to eat," said Kathryn with a firm tone.

"But she can hardly fit three people in her kitchen!" Turning again to Kristen, Dave continued, "Besides, you have no tax write-off without a mortgage."

Kristen put her arm around her sister's shoulders. "It's okay, Kathryn. I know that Dave means well. Dave, I always appreciate the offer. I'll let you know when I'm ready, okay? And it will probably be sooner than you think."

Dave looked at her quizzically, as Kristen continued. "But for now, let's eat this delicious dinner."

Brent and Melanie finally got their two active toddlers seated, as the rest were seated in their chairs. "Let's hold hands, as we say grace," said Dave. As they joined hands, Dave offered a prayer, thanking God for the blessed event of the birth of Jesus Christ, for their peace and freedom, and for the abundance that they enjoyed.

After dinner, the family gathered in the living room to exchange gifts. Kristen sat on the floor against the sofa with Squeak on her lap. Kathryn handed her a silver gift sack with green bows on it. "This is for you, Sis." Her kitten tried to peer into the sack. "It's from Dave and me."

Dave added, "I hope you'll take it the right way." Kristen looked puzzled, but began undoing the bows. Inside she found a soft, forest green sweater.

"Wow. This is gorgeous! And you know that I love green!"

"We're glad you like the sweater. But there's something else," said Kathryn hesitantly.

Kristen dug further into the sack, and found a rolled-up paper. Instantly, she knew that it was an architectural drawing. As she unrolled it, a floor plan for a house unfolded before. Dave cleared his throat. "I'm not trying to push you. This is just a suggestion."

Kristen got up and gave Dave and Kathryn a hug together. "Thanks to both of you. I love the sweater. And I'll study the floor plan. Dave, you're more like a brother than a brother-in-law. Thanks for looking after me."

"Okay, enough mush," interjected Brent. "Your nephews and niece went together on our present for you. We're not as rich, you know!" Brent grinned, and handed Kristen a rectangular box wrapped in bright red paper. Inside the box was a pair of plaid forest green slacks.

"They match the sweater!" announced Cydney. "And underneath, there's a toy for Squeak!"

Seth shook his head as he grinned. "Cydney never was good at keeping a secret."

"Well, the slacks are beautiful" Digging under the slacks, she found the present for Squeak, and tossed it to her. Her kitten began immediately rolling around on the floor with her green and blue ball. "And obviously Squeak loves the toy."

"Now let me hand out my gifts to each of you." Kristen gave her gifts first to the Brent and Melanie's children. They excitedly ripped off the wrapping paper, threw down their books, and started tearing into another present. "Aunt Kristen, thanks for the books. The kids really do love to be read to. We'll read to them later, " said Brent.

"Actually, I'd like to read to them."

Melanie enthusiastically responded, "They are all yours. You can take them home, too, if you want!"

Kristen held out a present to Brent and Melanie. "You might want to open this now."

"Pretty light, Kristen" said Brent as he shook the small box.

"Oh, Brent. Great gifts come in small packages," chided his wife gently.

They opened the box and took out a CD.

"Oh, it's Christmas music. Thanks, Aunt Kristen," said Brent.

"Actually, it's Christmas hymns to help us remember the real reason for celebrating this day," explained Kristen. "Melanie, you might want to read the enclosed card."

THE CHRISTMAS MESSENGER

"Okay. The card says: 'Free babysitting for the first weekend I'm off work.'" Melanie smiled and gleefully exclaimed, "Kristen, how wonderful!"

Brent laughed. "This is a joke, right?"

Melanie elbowed Brent. "It's not a joke. She's serious. I hope."

"Yes, of course I'm serious. Now dig further in the box."

"Oh, there's a gift certificate," said Brent excitedly. Let's see. It's for dinner. Where's 'Fernwood'? I've never heard of it. Have you, Melanie?"

"Isn't that the small restaurant on Jefferson Street?"

"Yes, that's the one. It's quiet and peaceful and they serve great food. I thought it would be a nice romantic place for the two of you, while I'm babysitting your children."

Brent looked quizzically at Kristen. "It's unlike you talk about romance—" His wife elbowed Brent again before he could finish.

"Kristen, this is so sweet of you! A romantic weekend by ourselves sounds wonderful! I love our children," Melanie said emphatically, while smiling at her children. The toddlers looked up from their playing, and smiled cherubically back at their mother. Then in a whisper she said, "But there are days when I just want to ship them to Jupiter!"

Kristen handed her present to Kathryn and Dave. "This one is for both of you."

Kathryn untied the ribbon and then gave the package to Dave to open. "Oh, it's a Christmas CD—"

"Let me guess. Christmas hymns to help us remember the true meaning of Christmas?" teased Dave with a smile.

"That's one of the attributes I like about you, Dave. You catch onto things so quickly," rebutted Kristen with a smile.

Kathryn put her arm around Dave's shoulders and smiled at her sister. "Well, we thank you. You're right that we need to stay focused on the real importance of this season." Reaching further into the box, she retrieved another gift. "Oh, Dave, look. There's also a beautiful photo album. How nice! We've kind of slacked off on taking pictures, but we'll get started again."

"Actually, it's a scrapbook for your favorite photos. It's only partially finished because I just came up with the idea last night—"

THE CHRISTMAS MESSENGER

Brent started laughing. "You just started your Christmas shopping last night!"

Kristen took a deep breath. "I don't know how to explain this. I finished my usual Christmas shopping last month. But I've been caring for this woman who's given me a different perspective on life and on Christmas. And after we talked yesterday afternoon, these ideas just came to me. Anyway, I started this scrapbook with pictures that I've taken of the family and special events during the past year. But I'm sure that you have some as well. Kathryn, I'll be happy to work with you on putting additional photos in this over the year."

"Well this is very thoughtful of you, Kristen," said Kathryn softly, while glancing through the pages. "Look, there are some pictures from last Christmas! And here are pictures from our Fourth of July picnic! My, how our grandchildren have grown!"

"Thanks" said Dave. "That's a great idea, although I was hoping for a tractor-mower!" he teased.

"When I win the Publisher's Clearinghouse $10 million award, I'll get you that tractor-mower. But you know the odds of that happening!" Turning towards her niece, she handed Cydney, a small gift sack. "Well, I know this isn't for scrapbooking or babysitting!" Cydney responded cheerfully. "But this is big enough for a CD!"

"Open it!" said her brothers, Brent and Seth, together.

Cydney opened the box, which contained a CD of Christmas hymns.

"Thanks for the Christmas <u>hymns</u>, Aunt Kristen. "You know I love Christmas music!"

"There's a card for you, too," added Kristen.

Cydney dug past the tissue paper. "Oh, here it is. It says, 'This card is exchangeable for lunch and an outfit of your choice during our shopping trip together!' Oh, thanks, Kristen. But I thought that you hated shopping!"

"Well, I know that you love to shop, and I wanted the two of us to do something that you would really enjoy."

Cydney jumped up and hugged her. "Thanks, Aunt Kristen. This shopping trip and lunch will be loads of fun!"

"Last but not least" said Kristen as she handed a gift to her nephew, Seth.

"I'll bet there's a CD in this," responded Seth with a grin.

"Of Christmas <u>hymns</u>," chimed in Brent and Dave, jovially.

"You know, Kristen, I've always wanted to spend some special time with you attending the Super Bowl!"

Kristen laughed. "Not on my salary!"

Seth unwrapped his gift. "Oh, look! A CD of Christmas hymns!" Seth paused, "Seriously, I really appreciate this. You wouldn't believe some of the music I've heard in the dorm this month."

Seth held the enclosed card. "So this isn't a trip with you to the Super Bowl?"

Kristen smiled and shook her head. "Sorry, it isn't."

"Okay. Seth ripped open the envelope dramatically. "And it reads, 'This card is exchangeable for lunch and a trip to the planetarium.' That's great! And there's a really awesome show at the planetarium now, which I haven't been able to go to because of finals."

"Let's play this Christmas CD while we have dessert," suggested Dave.

"Great idea," responded Kathryn. "I need some help getting things ready."

The group moved to the kitchen, gathering the decorated angel food cake and plates. In the dining room, the cake was sliced and passed to each.

"Why do we always have the same dessert each Christmas? Is this a family tradition from my great-great grandparents?" asked Seth.

Kathryn replied calmly, "Actually it's our family tradition. Angel food cake seems like the perfect food to be celebrating the birth of Jesus. What do you think of that?"

Seth nodded. "You're right. It is the perfect dessert for this special occasion!"

Melanie added, "I liked the idea so well, that Brent and I have it on Christmas Eve."

As they ate, they listened to the Christmas music. "What a great feeling of peace and love," said Kristen softly.

"That it is," replied Kathryn quietly. "And with this beautiful music, even the toddlers are subdued. It's wonderful having the family together to celebrate this special day. And Kristen, thanks for reminding us all about the real meaning of Christmas."

When dessert was over, Brent asked, "Well, Kristen, if you're serious about your offer, what weekend do you want the children?"

"How about the third weekend in January? That will give you a chance to recover from the holidays."

"It's a deal!" grinned Brent.

The toddlers had fallen asleep on the sofa. The rest of the family gathered around the fireplace, sipping hot chocolate, listening to Christmas music, and visiting. After awhile, Kristen had a feeling that she needed to go to the hospital. *This is strange. I've never felt compelled to return to the hospital after my shift. I hope this doesn't mean something bad.*

Kristen jumped up. "Well, I need to go. Thanks for a great Christmas!"

Kathryn and Dave looked surprised. "What's the hurry?" asked Kathryn.

"Sorry, I just feel that I need to go to the hospital to check on this patient," explained Kristen hurriedly.

Dave held Kristen's parka as she put it on. "You worry too much about your patients. That's the nice thing about being an architect."

Kathryn gave Kristen a hug. "Sorry that you have to leave so soon. We'll be thinking of you."

She bundled her kitten into her parka, gave a final wave to the family, and then jogged to her car. Looking up at the starry sky she remembered Emma's counsel: "Trust in God."

Driving to the hospital through empty streets, Kristen prayed out loud for Emma. "Dear God, Emma's taught me so much during the past few days. I'd hate to lose her at this point. But she's taught me to trust in Thee. So, I leave that decision in Thy hands. Please be with her, and bless us with Thy peace. Amen" A feeling of comfort and calmness came over Kristen. She didn't know if this was a good sign or not.

After parking in the nearly empty the hospital parking lot, she snuggled her kitten into her parka. "Squeak, you're not allowed in the hospital, but I can't leave you in my cold car. So, you need to be quiet, okay?" Squeak meowed softly. Once inside, she jogged down the hallway, and up the four flights of stairs to the MICU floor. Winded, she quickly walked through the automatic sliding doors and into the MICU, still wearing her parka. Esther, seated at the nurse's station, was startled to see her. "Kristen, what are you doing here?"

"Just felt that I needed to be with Emma," she responded quickly as she strode hurriedly to Emma's room.

At Emma's bedside, Kristen stood quietly, wanting to talk with her, but hesitant to awaken her. After a moment, Emma opened her eyes. "I thought that you might come. My, what an adorable kitten peeking out of your parka. I hope that you had a special Christmas with your family."

Kristen sat on the edge of the bed, and clasped her hands around Emma's hand. "I did. But I felt compelled to come and see you."

"It's always good to listening to those feelings. God often prompts us to action through gentle but persuasive impressions. Many times God answers his children's prayers through others. We must be willing to heed those divine promptings. Remember there aren't any coincidences in God's kingdom," replied Emma weakly.

Emma paused for a moment, and then looked intently at her. "Kristen, I know that all of us when we leave this Earth will be asked to account for our lives and behavior, and to account for our obedience to God's commandments. Accountability is so important in God's eternal plan. God wants us to overcome our imperfections and live righteously. He wants us to repent of our transgressions and move forward, becoming more and more virtuous. Promise me that you will remember that and share it with God's children."

"I promise. But this doesn't seem fair that you should go now."

Emma patted Kristen's hand. "It's time. I've accomplished what God wanted me to do. Remember: 'Life isn't fair, but—'

"'But God's love is always there. Turn to Him, and your pain will dim. Follow His light, and you will always be right.' I'll always remember that," she replied pensively.

"I won't need my hurricane lamp any more. Please take it with you, Kristen. You've been a great comfort to me in these past few days. Thanks for your kindness and loving care. When you go home, read John 14:27." whispered Emma weakly.

Kristen felt a lump in her throat and struggled to respond.

"Thanks for all you taught me. You've been a tremendous Christmas messenger teaching me about God's love and the real meaning of Christmas. Because of what you've shared, I had the most spiritual and memorable Christmas ever." Kristen brushed away her tears and then continued. "And I've grown closer to our Heavenly Father and to Jesus because of the truths that you have shared with me. I love you and I'll always remember you."

In a moment, Emma's eyes closed. Emma's hand went limp at the same time as her heart stopped beating on the monitor. Esther rushed in. Kristen responded quietly, "She signed a 'Do-Not-Resuscitate' order late this afternoon, so don't call the Code Team. I'd like to be alone with her for awhile."

"Sure, Kristen," Esther replied softly, and then left quickly.

She sat quietly, letting the tears flow, as she thought about Emma's life. "You've been through a lot, Emma. You've fought a valiant fight and lived a good life."

As though sensing something was wrong, Squeak gently licked Kristen's neck, and then purred softly. She cuddled her gratefully.

A few minutes later, Esther came to the doorway. "Kristen, I hate to disturb you, but there's a patient in the Emergency Department that needs to be transferred to the MICU." Esther hesitated. "We have no other beds."

Kristen brushed away her tears. "It's okay. I'm ready to leave."

"Do you want to notify her family?"

"There's no family."

"Oh. Well, okay then." Esther turned away and left.

Kristen picked up the hurricane lamp and walked slowly through the quiet hospital. Outside, in the cold night air, she shivered.

At home, Kristen turned on her gas log fire place and nestled onto her sofa. Squeak jumped up next to her, and snuggled on her lap. She opened her Bible and read John 14:27: "Peace I leave with you, my peace I give unto you: not as the world giveth, give I unto you. Let not your heart be troubled, neither let it be afraid."

"Dear God, if Emma is happy where she is now, please let me feel Thy peace."

Instantly, she felt a powerful comfort and peace replacing her grief. *This is amazing. This feeling must be from God because it certainly isn't from me.*

Then she pulled on her parka, tucked Squeak inside and walked outside her apartment. Outside in the quiet stillness of the late night, she looked upward at the black sky with its countless twinkling stars. "A new star heralded the birth of Jesus. I wonder what Emma is experiencing in heaven. I hope that it's glorious."

Then, remembering Emma's description, she knew in her heart of hearts that it was glorious beyond description.

Chapter Six

"My Peace I Give Unto You..."

On the last Sunday in April, Kristen was sitting in church next to a young couple.

With his arm gently encompassing his wife's shoulders, the man gazed lovingly at her as she cradled their infant in her arms. Kristen sighed before looking away. *I always wanted to marry, and to cradle my infant in my arms, but it never worked out.* And then she remembered Emma's counsel:

"Do your best, and trust in God for the rest."

She felt a combination of sorrow at the remembrance of Emma's death and gratitude for what Emma had shared with her. Suddenly she also felt strangely compelled to visit the grave sites of her parents and Emma. *I've never felt like this before. I always felt such sadness when I went to my parents' gravestones that I've avoided going.*

After the church service was over, she strolled outside. The warmth of the spring sunshine enveloped her as she recalled additional counsel from Emma: "Listen to those gentle promptings. They are from God."

Gazing up at the brilliantly blue sky, she finally surrendered herself to the prompting. "Okay, God. I don't understand, but I'll go," she whispered.

While driving across the valley to the oldest cemetery in the city, Kristen wondered about the meaning and wisdom of this unplanned visit. Even from a distance, the cemetery stood out because of the black, wrought iron fence surrounding it. Evergreen tress and lilac bushes lined the inside of the wrought iron fence, creating a park-like beauty. And in the spring, numerous bright yellow daffodils were on both sides of the narrow entrance, as if beckoning visitors to cross the threshold and pass through the wrought iron gate into the cemetery. *I'll go to my parents' grave sites first and then to Emma's*, she decided as she drove slowly along the narrow road. After parking, she felt a gnawing pain in her throat. "God, why did Thou bring me here?" Kristen whispered anxiously.

Stepping out of her car, Kristen could smell the sweet fragrances of the blossoming lilac bushes, mingled with evergreen trees. While searching for her parents' grave sites, she recollected another of Emma's lessons: "Have an attitude of gratitude."

Looking heavenward, she whispered, "Okay, there's no doubt about Thy wonderful creations. But I'd still rather not be here."

Kristen brushed off some dried leaves from her parents' grave markers. Suddenly she was recalling fond memories— skiing in the mountains, making smores at campfires, doing barbeques in the backyard, and many more. Instead of sadness, she felt consumed with joy. A half hour had passed as memories filled her heart with joy and indescribable peace. *This is truly amazing, because I've never felt such peace here before.*

Feeling completion with that part of her visit, she slowly strolled to Emma's grave site. There, she spoke softly, as though she was catching Emma up on her life. "Emma, I didn't know you for very long, but you taught me so much. Since your death, I've spent two weeks in central Africa being a nurse in the poorest hospital I've ever seen. And I've decided to expand my skills by getting my master's degree as a nurse practitioner. I'm rather nervous about leaving my comfort zone and starting a new career, but I'm mostly excited. I'll start classes next fall. I wouldn't have undertaken either goal without your guidance. And I'm working on becoming more spiritual. I read the scriptures and pray every day, which I never did before. I've even stopped swearing. Now, I recoil at even the thought of taking God or Christ's names in vain. I'm so very grateful that you shared so much of your life and wisdom with me."

Another half hour passed as she recalled memories and contemplated her life's goals. Finally, she looked up to the sky and whispered her heartfelt gratitude, "I feel such inexpressible joy. I thank Thee for prompting me to come!"

Enraptured with the feeling of peace that surpasses all understanding she gazed up with gratitude. *God's peace is indescribable!*

Although consumed with the warmth of His love, Kristen suddenly felt cold as a chilly wind abruptly started blowing and a gentle rain began to fall. Wearing only a short-sleeved dress, she hesitated only for a moment before dashing for the warmth of her car. In the distance she saw a man jogging to his minivan. Kristen had her hand on the car door handle when she felt compelled to look at the man again. *He looks familiar. Oh, he's the anesthesiologist whom I thought I recognized in the cafeteria last December. I still can't remember where I know him from. It must be from a long time ago.*

For some curious reason, she couldn't get the car door handle to open. She continued struggling with the handle, while looking at the man from her past. Then he noticed her. There was a momentary pause as their eyes met. Then he quickly got into his minivan and drove off. Immediately Kristen's car door opened, and she got in to escape from the chilly wind.

Although she had been planning to go home, she suddenly felt compelled to visit her sister, even though she lived in the opposite end of the valley. Kathryn looked surprised when she opened her front door and saw her. "Kristen, come in. We were just sitting down for some lunch. Come join us."

"Hey, Kristen, good to see you! This is my boyfriend, Trevor," bubbled her niece, Cydney, enthusiastically.

Kristen held out her hand to greet Trevor. "It's a pleasure to meet you." Still smiling and holding onto his hand, Kristen stated seriously, "You'd better be good to my only niece." Six feet tall and lanky, Trevor grinned, "Nice to meet you. Cydney is my best friend. I promise that I'll take good care of her!"

Kathryn added a place setting to the oak wood table in the dining room, as Cydney and Trevor brought the soup and sandwiches from the kitchen. Dave emerged from the family room. "Kristen, it's good to see you. How's work in the ICU?"

"Endless, of course. How's my number one brother-in-law?"

Dave chuckled. "Great! Relieved to hear that I'm still number one!"

They sat down, and joined hands, as Kathryn offered thanks to God and asked for His blessing on their meal.

"So, Kristen, when are you going to let me design a home for you? asked Dave earnestly. "I keep offering, just in case you ever change your mind."

"Actually, I was thinking of building a home this summer."

Silence quickly descended. Dave froze, while holding the plate of sandwiches. Trevor looked confused. "You've been in the same apartment for 10 years. What's happening?" asked Dave.

Cydney excitedly exclaimed , "You're finally going to build a house! That's so cool!"

Kristen didn't have a chance to respond before Kathryn interjected, "I'm so surprised! Have you looked at any lots?"

Kristen noticed that Trevor was staring at the plate of sandwiches that Dave was still holding. "Dave, perhaps you'd like to share those sandwiches. Trevor looks famished."

"Oh, sorry, Trevor," replied Dave as he passed the sandwiches. "It's just that I've been trying to talk Kristen into building a house for many years, and of course letting me design it. Her sudden change of heart rather astonishes me. So what's happened?"

"It's time. It's okay to be single and build your own home. And I want to be able to paint my walls any color I desire because I'm tired of white paint. And I'd like to put up some wallpaper. And I want to have enough sunlight inside that I can grow indoor plants. And I want an attached garage!"

"You still might get married!" bubbled Cydney.

"I guess that's always a possibility. But I have a lot of worthy goals to pursue. And I can find joy in achieving those goals."

"So are you going back to do nursing in Africa again?" asked Kathryn.

"Yes, and in other countries, too. There's great need in our hemisphere as well."

"Hey, after lunch, there's a lot in a great neighborhood that I want you to see." Dave interjected. "It's just a few blocks away. You would be closer to us, yet have about the same commute time to your work. It just became available, but it won't last that way for long. And I have some other floor plans for you to look at, too, in case you don't like the one I gave you at Christmas."

"Don't rush her," cautioned Kathryn.

"Rush her? I've waited about 20 years for her to make this decision!"

"Alright!" laughed Kristen. "Let's go look after we've finished eating!"

After lunch, Kristen went over some more of Dave's floor plans. "Just remember that I don't need a house as large as yours. There's only one of me."

"Okay. But what about when I want to send the kids and grandkids over to your home so we can have some peace and quiet?" Dave teased. "Anyway, these are smaller floor plans."

After spending several minutes studying the floor plans, they walked to the lot just four blocks away. "Isn't this a wonderful place to build a home?" asked Kathryn.

"It's beautiful!" replied Kristen enthusiastically.

"Nice view of the mountains," said Trevor quietly.

Cydney grabbed Kristen's hand and jogged with her across the lot. "Look at the great trees!"

"The trees are beautiful! Can we keep them rather than clearing the lot?" asked Kristen.

"We can arrange that," answered Dave. "And it's a superb neighborhood."

"It would be awesome to have you so close!" exclaimed Cydney.

Kathryn put her arm around Kristen's shoulders. "This is a big step for you, Sis. Don't feel like you need to rush into it."

Dave interjected, "She's not rushing! Besides, this is an excellent lot and it won't be on sale for long. Why don't you take the copies of the floor plans home with you, and give me a call later? If you really want this lot, you should consider putting earnest money down quickly."

"Thanks, Dave, for sharing your architect skills with me."

"Sharing your talents with one another is one of the joys of being a family. However—and don't take this wrong—I hope that we don't need your ICU skills!"

"Understood. Well, I'd better get home and do some serious thinking."

The family waved as she drove off in her older model sedan. "Now all we need to do is convince her to buy a red sports car," teased Cydney.

"One thing at a time, but I don't think a red sports car fits her personality" replied Dave. "Building a house is a big step for her. I wonder what really changed her mind."

Cydney grabbed Trevor's hand and giggled, "Maybe she actually does have a boyfriend but she doesn't want to tell us!"

Kathryn chided them. "Oh, come now. I would know if my sister had a boyfriend."

Before her alarm went off the next morning, Kristen was wide awake. *If I'm this full of energy, I might as well go for a run!* She pulled on her navy jogging suit. As she sat on her bed tying her shoes, Squeak jumped up bedside her. "You grow bigger each month," she said, while gently stroking her kitty.

She cradled Squeak in her arms as she got up. Before leaving her bedroom, she gazed for a moment at Emma's hurricane lamp with its gleaming gold base, next to the gold box with her Christmas gifts to Jesus. She touched them. Then she bowed her head, closed her eyes and softly prayed, "God, I'm thankful for the lessons Emma taught me about life and Thee. As for the resolutions on self-improvement that I made last Christmas, I've made some progress, but I have a lot of work to do. Please help me to continue in my efforts, I pray name in the name of thy beloved Son, Jesus. Amen"

In the kitchen, she drank a glass of orange juice and ate a banana. Squeak playfully batted a ball around on the floor. She gave Squeak a hug, opened her front door and then slipped into the stillness of the early morning. She jogged for a half an hour in the placidity of a nearby park. As the sun rose enveloping the valley in a warm glow, she stopped to gaze upwards for a moment at the sunlight filtering through the trees that encompassed the park. Wanting to stay, but knowing that she needed to get ready for work, she turned around and jogged back to her home. A quick shower relaxed her muscles. With a little time to spare, she decided to eat at the hospital.

In the cafeteria, Kristen was eating her blueberry bagel when she saw him again—the doctor from her past, with the dark brown, wavy hair. As before, he was looking at her, while paying for his breakfast. *I guess I'll never know who he is because he always looks away.*

She took another bite of her bagel, and then she was shocked to see him walking towards her table. "Mind if I join you?" he asked in a soft voice.

Kristen gulped down her mouthful of bagel and stammered, "Uuh, yes. I mean no, I don't mind—"

And then she remembered. "You're Joel Radcliff! How many years has it been since we were in high school together?"

"Well, there have been at least two of those ten-year high school reunions. Do you want me to be more specific?" Joel smiled shyly and then they both laughed.

"I recognized you last December, but I guess you didn't recognize me?" Joel asked.

Kristen stammered again, and finally admitted the truth. "I just knew that I knew you, but from where I couldn't recall. But you didn't wear glasses or have any grey hairs back in high school. You also have a better memory than me. I would have never survived senior year biology without your help as my lab partner."

"That was a tough course. But looking back, high school was a pretty halcyon time."

She nodded in agreement. "I suppose it was, compared to what both you and I have seen working in a hospital. You know, it was your discussions about medicine that inspired me to pursue a career in nursing. But I'm surprised that you're an anesthesiologist rather than a surgeon considering how well you did at dissecting."

Joel pushed up his wire-rimmed glasses and said softly, "When you're as shy as I've always been, it's easier being an anesthesiologist."

"Well, I suppose you've got a valid point there."

There was an awkward silence, which they filled with chewing.

Then Joel blurted out, "Did you know I always wanted to date you in high school?"

Kristen stopped chewing and stared at Joel. Gulping once again, she responded, "And I always wanted to date you."

Joel stared in disbelief. "You did?"

"Of course, but I was rather shy myself, so I guess I didn't know how to let you know. But why didn't you ask me out?"

Joel looked down at his plate for a moment, and then looked earnestly at Kristen. "I was too afraid that you would turn me down. And I couldn't handle that, especially with you being my lab partner. So, what happened to you after high school, besides becoming an ICU nurse. I noticed that you're not wearing a wedding ring, but—well, I'm certain that you've been married. I hope that I'm not out of line," he stammered.

Kristen sighed and quickly explained,. "I've never been married. There aren't enough men. Now, what about you? The last I knew, you were dating a girl who was a junior."

"That was Maureen." Joel paused and stared out the window for a moment before looking back at Kristen. "My sister arranged for us to double-date. Without my sister's help I probably would have never dated. But Maureen's enthusiasm compensated for my quiet nature. She became my best friend. We dated for another year when she joined me at the university and then we were married—"

"I didn't know that you married so young!"

"Well, it was common for our classmates and friends to live together before getting married. But Maureen and I wanted to obey God's commandments." Joel wavered before proceeding. "By then we had dated for two years and we just knew that we were meant for each other. I don't know how you now feel about God and religion, but we believed in celibacy before marriage, and totally fidelity after. That wasn't a popular concept then and is less so now." Joel hesitated.

Kristen felt amazed. "You know, Joel, a few months ago, I thought I was the only one left who felt that way. But since then, I've learned that I'm not alone."

Joel nodded his head slowly. "Anyway, we chose to marry young and then start a family. When I finished my residency in Charleston, we stayed there because Maureen played cello for the symphony and just loved it there. She also was a gifted singer and sang in our church choir." Joel paused once again and stared out the window. "Unfortunately, Maureen didn't like to wear a seat belt. She would wear it when the children or I were in the car. But she wasn't wearing it when she was alone and a drunk driver came across the median." Joel looked out the window again. His voice quivered as he continued. "Her death was an indescribable loss for the family." Joel quickly brushed his cheeks with his hand. After a moment, he turned his face back to Kristen. "Over the past 13 months we've slowly been healing. We moved back here last summer so that the children could be close to their grandparents."

Kristen was stunned with the news. But she felt calmness, like she had experienced recently at the cemetery. Then she remembered seeing Joel there and the chilly wind that caused their paths to cross. *That's an amazing coincidence.* Immediately Kristen remembered Emma saying, "There are no coincidences in God's kingdom."

With tear-filled eyes, Kristen quietly responded, "My heart grieves for you." She brushed away her own tears. "I was at church last Sunday, when I felt prompted to go to the cemetery. My parents and a friend are buried there. I didn't want to go, but I felt compelled to do so. It's the only time that I've felt such peace, and even joy just recalling fond memories. Someday I'm sure that you'll feel that, too. It's difficult to explain. I've also found great comfort in John 14:27. Are you familiar with that scripture?"

Joel nodded. "Yes. 'God's peace surpasses all understanding.' It's strange how you can feel such tremendous sadness being replaced by peace. When I saw you at the cemetery, I was surprised. But at that moment, I somehow knew that you would have empathy with what we've gone through."

Kristen suddenly remembered Emma's lamp. Impulsively she said, "There's something I want you to have that will remind you of God's infinite love. It's a hurricane lantern with a card that reads: 'Life isn't fair, but God's love is always there. Turn to Him, and your pain will dim. Follow His light, and you will eternally be right.' Someday I'll tell you the story behind that lamp and verse. But for now, I think you should have it as a reminder of God's infinite love during your healing process."

Joel furrowed his eyebrows and looked pensively at Kristen. "Let me know if I got that saying right: 'Life isn't fair, but God's love is always there—"

Kristen filled in the rest. "Turn to him and your pain will dim. Follow His Light, and you will eternally be right."

"There's an abundance of truth to that saying. Thanks for sharing that with me."

Then Kristen remembered their eyes meeting at the cemetery, followed by Joel's abrupt departure. "So, why did you leave the cemetery so hurriedly after you saw me?"

"Well, I'd been at a meeting at my church, and was on my way home, when I felt compelled to go to the cemetery. So I went there for a few minutes. But my children had already gone home and were getting lunch ready." Joel smiled, "Besides, my four teenagers wouldn't wait for long before eating everything in sight!"

"Four teenagers!" exclaimed Kristen in disbelief.

Joel grinned as he reached for his wallet. Pulling out a worn picture of his family, Joel proudly pointed out each child. "Nathan is 17, and a senior. Peter is 15, and a sophomore. There are our 13 year old twins—Michelle and Monica."

"They're beautiful children!"

Joel's beeper suddenly went off, startling them both. He looked at the digital display. "Oh, it's the OR. Sorry, but I need to go."

"I'll go with you. It's time for me to get to the MICU."

They deposited their trays and walked in silence to the stairs. She looked up at Joel, who was almost a foot taller. "I always take the stairs."

"I do too," replied Joel. "But it's hard to talk when you do. Besides the elevator is already here."

There were only a couple of people in the elevator, but more followed them, squeezing Joel and Kristen closer together than they had ever experienced before. Neither could think of anything to say while they were packed together like sardines. At the fourth floor, they both got off and walked in silence down the corridor. At the entrance to the MICU, Joel looked pensively at Kristen, as though searching for the right words.

"Thanks. Hope to see you around," he blurted out. Quickly he turned away and dashed down the hall towards the operating suite.

Startled with his hasty exit, Kristen finally exclaimed, "Bye, Joel. Nice seeing you again."

Joel stopped outside the OR, turned and waved quickly, and then vanished behind the automatic sliding door.

Kristen stared at the OR, feeling both confused and sad. She was startled to hear Anna behind her. "Kristen, do you have a boyfriend you haven't told us about?" she teased with a grin.

She wasn't prepared to deal with any friendly teasing. Her heart ached from the attraction to Joel that she had buried long ago, as well as from the sorrow that Joel and his children had experienced. *Dear God, please help me to know how to help Joel.* Almost immediately, she felt the ache in her heart being replaced with peace.

Turning towards Anna and the MICU, she responded simply, "He's just a friend from high school. This is the first I've talked with him since graduation." Then she turned and walked through the MICU doors to begin her work.

Her shift about over, Kristen was sitting alone in the small computer area adjacent to the nurses' station. As she finished her last chart, she logged off the computer, looked up and saw the automatic doors opened just as Joel walked in. *I've never seen him here before. I wonder if he's going to ask me out. No, that's idiotic! He's probably just checking on a patient.*

Kristen watched as Joel walked to the nurses' station, picked up some papers and then came into the computer area. He looked for a second at her, smiled weakly and uttered a soft "Hello". He then sat down and intently studied the papers.

Kristen tried to not gaze at Joel and tried to look busy herself, even though she was finished with her charting. *His behavior is so peculiar. Dear God, men are the strangest creatures on Earth. Well, maybe not the strangest—but certainly incomprehensible at times. Oh, what's the use of praying? Gender-bias has probably existed since Adam. No, I can't really believe that God is biased towards men. And, I certainly haven't succeeded on my own, so maybe I should try praying anyway.* She stopped and took a deep breath before praying silently. *"Heavenly Father, I'm sorry for doubting Thy unconditional love for all Thy children. I just don't know what to do or what to say to Joel. Please guide me. Amen."*

Suddenly, Kristen recalled the evenings that she had spent with Joel quizzing each other in preparation for their biology tests. After preparing for their tests, Joel's mother would bake for them his favorite meal of Hawaiian pizza with pineapple and ham. *Maybe I could invite him over for pizza. No, that's a foolish idea! He'll think I'm too forward, or something.*

But the thought just kept persisting. Joel was still intently studying the same papers. And then Kristen realized that he was just staring at an insurance page. *Well, he certainly doesn't need to know anything about any patient's insurance. Maybe he did come here to talk to me.*

Her heart began pounding rapidly and loudly. She gulped and said, "Joel—"

Just then, Rebecca and Karen came to the nurses' station talking about a patient who needed to be admitted. A group of doctors making rounds came through the MICU doors, with the faculty physician talking enthusiastically about genetic engineering as they approached the nurses' station. The evening shift of nurses was also descending upon the nurses' station as well as the computer area.

Joel looked cautiously at Kristen and saw her looking carefully at him. He tilted his head towards the MICU doors. She nodded and smiled. Without a word, they got up and walked out of the MICU together. In silence they walked to the end of corridor next to a window that offered a beautiful view of the valley.

"What were you going to say?" he asked hesitantly, gazing at her for only a second before looking out the window.

Kristen's heart was still pounding so loudly that she figured even Joel could hear it. As Kristen recalled that he'd seemingly taken a risky step that morning by just sitting at her table, she cleared her throat and took a deep breath. And then she plunged forward, "Well, I was just wondering if you still liked pizza as much as you used to?"

The tension in Joel's face eased completely and he quickly responded, "You bet!" he said as he looked directly at her.

She took another deep breath and plunged ahead, hoping that the memory was actually divine inspiration. "I'm off work this coming Saturday. Would you like to come over and we'll make a pineapple and ham pizza just like your mother did for us so long ago?"

Joel breathed an audible sigh of relief as he smiled. "How wonderful that you remembered my favorite meal after all those years! And thanks for the invitation. I'd love to come," he said with his characteristic gentle enthusiasm.

Joel's words filled her with a tenderness and warmth that she hadn't experienced since he was her biology lab partner. Then she recalled the love poem that Emma had shared with her. She felt like she should share it, even though the thought of doing so pushed her far beyond her comfort zone. But the feeling wouldn't leave. Hesitantly, she said, "I not only liked you a lot in high school, but I respected and trusted you. You remind me of a poem that I've found so meaningful, but I never thought it would apply to my life."

"Please share it with me," asked Joel softly.

"Okay, but I hope you won't think it's too sappy."

"I promise I won't," he said kindly.

"Well, alright." Taking a deep breath, Kristen proceeded, almost in a whisper. "I only remember the first part of it, but it begins like this: 'I love you not only for what you are, but for what I am when I am with you. I love you not only for what you have made of yourself, but what you are making of me...'"Then her mind went blank.

Joel smiled, and tenderly held Kristen's hand. "I can finish it for you. 'You have done it without a touch, without a word, without a sign. You have done it by being yourself. Perhaps that is what being a friend means after all.' Kristen, you were a wonderful friend to me in high school. Can we pick up where we were so many years ago?"

She breathed a sigh of relief. "I think we're already way ahead of where we were in high school."

Just at that moment, Joel's pager went off. They both jumped. He rolled his eyes in exasperation as he slide the pager out of its holder and looked at the number. "It's the OR. It must be an emergency case. Will you walk with me there?"

"Of course."

Joel put his arm across Kristen's shoulders. "So what kind of hobbies do you enjoy?"

"Repelling used to be my favorite sport, which I was planning on restarting again."

Kristen saw Joel grimace.

"Still a bit fearful of heights? "

"I love hiking up mountains or skiing down mountains. I just don't want to be hanging from a cliff. Would you consent to hiking rather than repelling?' Joel asked with a smile.

"Absolutely! Maybe we can hike up to Crystal Lake with your children later this month."

Joel gently hugged her with one arm already around her shoulders, "They would love it."

At the entrance to the OR, Joel waved and dashed in. Kristen waved back and watched until she could no longer see him through the glass window. For a moment she thought about the amazing events of the day. *I can't believe that so much has changed in a matter of one day!* As she walked outside into the sunlight, Kristen glanced upwards and offered a silent prayer of gratitude. She knew in her heart of hearts that her life—and Joel's—had changed forever. A thrill of emotion consumed her, the same as during her high school years with Joel. She felt part school girl and part mature woman. But besides the thrill of romance, Kristen realized a sense of humble gratefulness at the divine intercession that had kindled pure love and changed the course of her life.

THE END.

www.ingramcontent.com/pod-product-compliance
Ingram Content Group UK Ltd.
Pitfield, Milton Keynes, MK11 3LW, UK
UKHW041954230426
12048UKWH00008B/329